"He's your whole existence, isn't he?"

Wanda didn't wait for an answer as she continued cruelly, "You're such a fool, Florina. Just because Sir William treats you decently and appears to take an interest in you. Don't you know that that's part of his work—being kind and turning on the charm for hysterical mothers?"

"That's not true," Florina interrupted Sir William's fiancée angrily. "Sir William is kind and good and he loves his work. Say what you like about me, but you're not going to say a word against him!"

"Oh, Lord, you're so funny." Wanda laughed. "If only you could see that plain face of yours. Well, you're only his cook, and not for much longer!"

Florina left the room, shaking with rage and filled with only one thought: Wanda was so wrong for the man Florina knew and loved.

Betty Neels is well-known for her romances set in the Netherlands, which is hardly surprising. She married a Dutchman and spent the first twelve years of their marriage living in Holland and working as a nurse. Today she and her husband make their home in a small ancient stone cottage in England's West Country, but they return to Holland often. She loves to explore tiny villages and tour privately owned homes there, in order to lend an air of authenticity to the locales of her books.

Books by Betty Neels

HARLEQUIN ROMANCE

2666—ONCE FOR ALL TIME
2680—HEIDELBERG WEDDING
2692—YEAR'S HAPPY ENDING
2712—A SUMMER IDYLL
2729—AT THE END OF THE DAY
2741—MAGIC IN VIENNA
2752—NEVER THE TIME AND THE PLACE
2787—A GIRL NAMED ROSE
2808—TWO WEEKS TO REMEMBER
2824—THE SECRET POOL
2855—STORMY SPRINGTIME
2874—OFF WITH THE OLD LOVE
2891—THE DOUBTFUL MARRIAGE

Harlequin Books

TORONTO • NEW YORK • LONDON
AMSTERDAM • PARIS • SYDNEY • HAMBURG
STOCKHOLM • ATHENS • TOKYO • MILAN

Original hardcover edition published in 1987
by Mills & Boon Limited

ISBN 0-373-02914-4

Harlequin Romance first edition June 1988

Printed in U.S.A.

CHAPTER ONE

THE hot June sunshine of a late afternoon bathed the narrow country road in warmth, and the only traveller on it dawdled along, pedalling slowly, partly from tiredness after a day's work, and partly from a reluctance to arrive at her home.

The village came in sight round the next curve: the bridge over the river, leading to the road which would eventually join the high road to Salisbury, and then the cottages on either side of the lane. They were charming, tiled or thatched, their red bricks glowing in the sunshine, their porches wreathed with clematis and roses. The cyclist came to a halt before one of these, and at the same time a silver-grey Bentley swam to a soundless halt beside her.

The girl got off her bike. She was small and thin, with gingery hair plaited into a thick rope over one shoulder, green eyes transforming an ordinary face into something which, while not pretty, certainly lifted it from the ordinary.

The car driver got out: a very large man, towering over her. Not so young, she decided, studying him calmly, but very good-looking, with dark hair sprinkled with grey, a formidable nose and heavy-lidded blue eyes. He smiled down at her, studying her in his turn, and then dismissing her from his thoughts. None the less, he smiled at her and his deep voice was pleasant.

'I wonder if you could help us? We wanted to stay the night in the village, but the Trout and Feathers can't put us up and we would rather not drive back to Wilton or Salisbury.' He glanced over his shoulder to where a small girl's face was thrust through the open window of the car. 'Just bed and breakfast—we can get a meal at the pub.'

He held out a hand. 'The name is Sedley—William Sedley.'

The girl offered a small brown hand and had it engulfed. 'Florina Payne, and yes, if you go on as far as the bridge, there is a farmhouse facing it; they haven't got a board up, but I'm sure they would put you up.' She wrinkled her ginger brows. 'There isn't anybody else in the village, I'm afraid. You would have to go back to Burford St Martin on the main road.'

She was thanked politely, and the child in the front seat waved to her as they drove off. She wheeled her bike along the brick path at the side of the cottage and went in through the kitchen door, thinking about the driver of the car, to have her thoughts rudely shattered by her father's voice.

'So there you are—took your time coming home, didn't you? And then wasted more of it talking to that fellow. What did he want, anyway?'

The speaker came into the kitchen, a middle-aged man with an ill-tempered face. 'You might at least get home punctually; you know I can't do anything much for myself, and here I am, alone all day and you crawling back when it suits you . . .'

He paused for breath and Florina said gently, 'Father, I came just as soon as I could get off. The hotel is very busy with the tourist season, you know, and that man only wanted to know where he could get a room for the night.'

Her father snorted. 'Pah, he could afford a hotel in Wilton, driving a Bentley!' He added spitefully, 'Wasting your time and his for that matter—who'd want to look twice at a ginger-headed plain Jane like you?'

Florina was laying the table and, although colour stole into her cheeks, she answered in a matter-of-fact voice. 'Well, it won't be a waste of time if he gets a room at the farm. Sit down, Father, tea won't be long.'

She would very much have liked to have sat down herself and had a cup of tea; it had been a busy day at the hotel. During the summer season, tourists expected meals at odd hours, and she and the other two cooks there had worked all day, whisking up omelettes, steaks, fish dishes, egg dishes and salads, just as fast as they could. They had taken it in turn to eat a sandwich and drink a mug of tea, but it had been a long day. She had worked there for three years now, hating the long cycle ride in the winter to and from her home, as well as the long hours and the lack of free time. But the pay, while not over-generous, was good; it supplemented her father's pension and brought him all the extra comforts he took as his right. That it might have given her the chance to buy pretty clothes had never entered his head; she was his daughter, twenty-seven years old, on the plain side, and it was her duty to look after him while he lived. Once or twice she had done her best to break free, and each time, when she had confronted him with a possible job away from home, he had clutched at his chest, gasped that he was dying and taken to his bed. A dutiful, but not loving daughter—for what was there to love?—she had accepted that after the one heart attack he had had several years ago, he could have another if he became upset or angry; so she had given in.

She was a sensible girl and didn't allow self-pity to overwhelm her. She was aware that she had no looks to speak of, and those that she had were hardly enhanced by the cheap clothes, bought with an eye to their hard-wearing quality rather than fashion.

Her father refused to cook for himself during the day. She left cold food ready for him before she left each morning, and tea was a substantial meal, which meant that she had to cook once more. Haddock and poached eggs, a plate of bread and butter, stewed fruit and custard, and tea afterwards. She had no appetite for it, but the suggestion that they might have salads and cold meat met with a stream of grumbles, and anything was better than that after a day's work.

They ate in silence. Her father had no interest in her day and, since he had done nothing himself, there was nothing to tell her. He got up from the table presently and went into the sitting-room to sit down before the TV. Florina started to clear the table, wash up and put everything ready for breakfast. By the time she had finished the evening was well advanced but still light; half an hour's walk would be pleasant, she decided. She cheerfully countered her father's objections to this and set off through the village, past the cottages, past the Trout and Feathers, past the lovely old house next the pub where old Admiral Riley lived, and along the tree-lined lane. It was still warm and very quiet, and if she stood still she could hear the river beyond the trees.

When she came to a gate she stopped to lean on it, well aware of the beauty of her surroundings, but too busy with her own thoughts to heed it. The need to escape was very strong; her mother had died five years previously and since then Florina had kept house for her father, pandering to his whims, because the doctor had warned her that a fit of temper or any major disturbance might bring on another heart attack. She had resigned herself to what was her plain duty, made the more irksome since her father had no affection for her. But things could be different now; her father had been for a check-up in Salisbury a week or so previously and, although he had told her that there was no improvement in his condition, she had quite by chance encountered the doctor, who had told her that her father was fit enough to resume a normal life.

'A part-time job, perhaps?' He smiled at Florina, whom he thought privately had had a raw deal. 'He was in a bank, wasn't he? Well, I dare say he could get taken on again. He's only in his mid-fifties, isn't he? And if he can't find something to do, I've suggested to him that he might take over the housework; a little activity would do him good. Give you a chance to have a holiday.'

She mulled over his news. Her father had flown into a rage when she had suggested that he might like to do a few chores around the house. He had clutched his chest and declared that she would be the death of him, and that she was the worst possible daughter that any man could have.

Florina, having heard it all before, received his remarks with equanimity and said no more, but now she turned over several schemes in her mind. A different job, if she could find one and, since her father no longer was in danger, preferably away from home. Something not too far away, so that she could return for the weekends . . . She was so deep in thought that she didn't hear anyone in the lane until they were almost level with her. The man and the little girl from the car, walking along hand in hand. When she turned to see who it was, the man inclined his head gravely and the little girl grinned and waved. Florina watched them walk on, back to the village. Presumably they had found their bed and breakfast, and tomorrow they would drive away in their lovely car and she would never see them again.

She waited until they were out of sight, and then started back to the house. She had to leave home just after seven each morning, and tomorrow it would be even earlier, for there was a wedding reception at the hotel.

She went back without haste, made their evening drinks, wished her father goodnight and went to her room, where she wasted five minutes examining her features in the looking-glass. There was, she considered, very little to be done about them: sandy hair, even though it gleamed and shone, was by no means considered beautiful, and a slightly tip-tilted nose and too wide a mouth held no charm. She got into bed and lay wondering about the man in the car. He had been very polite in a disinterested way; she could quite see that there was nothing in her person to attract a man, especially a man such as he, used, no doubt, to enchanting girls with golden hair and beautiful faces, wearing the latest fashions. Florina smiled at her silly thoughts and went off to sleep.

It was the beginning of the most gorgeous day when she left early the next morning. Sir William Sedley, standing at his bedroom window and drinking his early morning tea, watched her pedalling briskly along the lane. The sun shone on her sandy head, turning it to gold, and she was whistling. He wondered where she was going at that early hour. Then he forgot her, almost immediately.

It was a splendid morning and there was almost no traffic. Florina, going at a great rate on her elderly bike, wished that she could have been free to spend the day out of doors. The hotel kitchens, admirable though they were, were going to be uncomfortably warm. She slowed a little as she went through the small town, still quiet, and passed the nice old houses with the high walls of Wilton House behind them. The hotel was on the other side of the road, a pleasant building, surrounded by trees and with the river close by. She paused to take a look at the green peacefulness around her, then parked her bike and went in through the kitchen entrance.

She was punctual, as always, but the place was already a hive of activity; first breakfasts being cooked, waiters loading trays. Florina called 'good morning' and went over to her particular corner, intent on icing *petits fours*, filling vol-au-vents and decorating the salmon in aspic designed for the wedding reception.

She was a splendid cook, a talent she had inherited from her Dutch mother, together with a multitude of housewifely perfections which, sadly, her father had never appreciated. Florina sometimes wondered if her mother had been happy; she had been a quiet little woman, sensible and practical and cheerful, absorbing her father's ill-temper with apparent ease. Florina missed her still. Whether her father did so too, she didn't know, for he never talked of her. When, from time to time, she had tried to suggest a holiday with her mother's family, he had been so incensed that he had become alarmingly red in the face, and she had feared that he would have another heart attack.

Her thoughts, as busy as her fingers, darted to and fro, seeking an escape from a home which was no longer a home. Interlarded with them was the man in the car, although what business of his it was eluded her.

He wasn't thinking of her; he was strolling down the village street, his daughter beside him. His appointment was for ten o'clock and it wanted five minutes to the hour. The church clock struck the hour as they turned in through the open gates leading to the house where Admiral Riley lived.

It was a delightful place, L-shaped, its heavy wooden door half-way down one side. It stood open, and there was no need to thump the great knocker, for the old man came to meet them.

'Mrs Birch from the village, who looks after me while my wife is away, has gone to Wilton. So I'm alone, which is perhaps a good thing, for we can go round undisturbed.'

He led the way through the hall and into a very large room with a window at its end. There were more windows and an open door along one side. It was furnished with some handsome mahogany pieces, and a number of easy chairs, and there was a massive marble fireplace facing the windows. The admiral went across the room and bent down to roll back the carpet before the hearth.

'I don't know if the agent told you about this?' He chuckled and stood back so that his visitors could see what he had laid bare. A thick glass panel in the floor, and under it a steady flow of water. 'There used to be a mill wheel, but that's gone. The water runs under this room...' He led the way through the doors on to a wide patio and leaned over a stone balustrade. 'It comes out here and runs through the garden into the fields beyond.'

The little girl caught her father's hand. 'Swans, Daddy!' Her voice was a delighted squeak. 'Do they live here, in this garden?'

'Not quite in the garden,' said the Admiral. 'But they come for bread each day. You shall feed them presently, if you like.'

The kitchen wing was in the other side of the L-shape, a delightful mixture of old-fashioned pantries, with everything that any housewife could wish for. There were other rooms, too: a dining-room, a small sitting-room, a study lined with bookshelves. Upstairs, the rooms were light and airy; there were five of them and three bathrooms, as well as a great attic reached by a narrow little stair. 'My playroom,' whispered the little girl.

They went back to the drawing-room presently, and the Admiral fetched the coffee tray and bread for the swans. 'I've been here for more than twenty years,' he observed, 'and we hate to leave it, but my wife has to live in a warm climate. She's been in Italy for a couple of months and already she is greatly improved. May I ask where you come from, Sir William?'

'London—Knightsbridge. I'm a paediatrician, consultant at several hospitals. I want Pauline to grow up in the country and, provided I can get help to run the house, I can drive up and down to town and stay overnight when I must. There's a good school, I hear; Pauline can go by the day.'

'Too far for her to cycle.'

'Yes, whoever comes here to look after us will have to drive her in and fetch her each day. A problem I'll deal with later.' He smiled suddenly. 'I should like to buy your house, Admiral. May our solicitors get to work on it?'

He sat back in his chair, very relaxed, a calm man who had made up his mind without fuss. 'They'll take three weeks if we bully them,' he said. 'May I come again with someone to advise me about cooking stoves and so on?' He added, 'I'm a widower, but I have plans to re-marry.'

'Of course. I shall probably be ready to move out before the solicitors fix a date. Feel free to arrange for carpets and curtains and so forth. Wilton is small, but there are a couple of excellent furnishing firms.'

They finished their coffee in companionable silence; two men who arranged their lives without fuss.

Walking back through the village, presently, Sir William asked, 'You're pleased, darling? You'll be happy here? I'll get Nanny to come and live with us for a time...'

'Until you marry Miss Fortesque?' said Pauline in a sad voice, so that her father stopped to look down at her.

'Look, darling, I know it's a bit difficult for you to understand, but Wanda is very fond of you, and it'll be nice for you to have someone to come home to and talk to...'

'There's you, Daddy...'

'I shall be in town for several days in the week. Once Wanda's here she will be able to get to know everyone about, and you'll have lots of friends.'

Pauline's small, firm mouth closed into an obstinate line. 'I'd be quite happy with Nanny.'

'Yes, love, but Nanny retired last year, she won't want to start working all over again. If she comes for a few months...'

'Until you get married?'

'Until I get married,' repeated her father gently, and then, 'I thought you liked Wanda?'

Pauline shrugged her small shoulders. 'She's all right, but she's not like a mother, is she? She fusses about her clothes!'

'I imagine you'll fuss about yours when you're older. Now, what shall we do with the rest of our day?'

He drove her to Stourhead and they had lunch at the Spread Eagle pub. Then they wandered right round the lake, and on the way back in the afternoon they stopped in Shaftesbury and had a cream tea. It was well past six o'clock before they got back to the farm. It was a warm evening and the country was very beautiful; they wandered over the road to the bridge and leaned over to watch the river, waiting until their evening meal would be ready. The church clock struck seven as they left the bridge and strolled to the road. They had to wait a moment while a cyclist went by.

'That's the nice girl we saw yesterday,' said Pauline.

'Was she nice?' asked Sir William in an uninterested manner.

Pauline nodded her head vigorously. 'Oh, yes. When we live here I shall ask if I may be her friend.'

'A bit old for you, darling?' He had no idea of the girl's age, and he wasn't interested. 'You must go to bed directly after supper. We're going to make an early start in the morning.'

They were driving through Wilton when Pauline saw the small, ginger-haired figure getting off her bike as they passed the hotel. 'Oh, there she is!' she cried excitedly. 'Daddy, do you suppose she works there?'

Sir William glanced sideways without slackening speed. 'Very likely. I dare say you'll see more of her when we come to live here.'

It was July when Admiral Riley left, and after that there was a constant coming and going of delivery vans, carpet layers, plumbers and painters. The village, via the Trout and Feathers, knew all that was going on and, naturally enough, Florina knew too. The new owner would move in in two weeks' time, his small daughter was going to school in Wilton, and there was a housekeeper coming. Also, Mrs Datchett from Rose Cottage, and Mrs Deakin, whose husband was a farm worker, were to go to work there four times a week.

'Disgraceful,' grumbled Florina's father. 'That great house, with just a man and child in it . . .'

'But there's work for Mrs Datchett and Mrs Deakin, close to their own homes, as well as for old Mr Meek, who is seeing to the garden. And the tradespeople—it's much better than leaving the house empty, Father.'

'Don't talk about things you don't understand,' snapped Mr Payne. 'It's bad enough that you go gallivanting off to work each day, leaving me to manage as best I can . . .'

Florina, laying the table for their meal, wasn't listening. She had heard it all before. It was wicked, she supposed, not to love her father, but she had tried very hard and been rebuffed so often that she had given up. Once or twice she had questioned the amount of her wages which he told her were necessary to supplement his income, only to be told to mind her own business. And she had done so, under the impression that his health would suffer if she thwarted him. Now according to the doctor, there was no longer any fear of that.

She went into the kitchen to cook the liver and bacon. Moments later her father poked his head round the door and demanded to know if he was to get anything to eat. 'I dare say you'd like to see me dead,' he grumbled.

'No, Father, just a bit more cheerful,' said Florina. At the same time, she resolved to start looking for another job on the very next day.

As it happened, she had no need. She was getting on her bike the next morning when Mrs Datchett came out of Rose Cottage, just across the street, and accosted her.

'Eh, love, can you spare a minute? You've heard I'm to go up to the Wheel House to work? Well, the housekeeper who took me on asked me if I knew of a good cook, and I thought of you. Lovely kitchen it is, too, and a cushy job as you might say, with that Sir William away most of the time and only the little girl and that housekeeper there. I don't know what he'll pay, but you'd not have that bike ride every day. Why don't you have a go?'

Florina cycled to work, thinking hard. By the time she got there she had made her mind up to apply for the job; it could do no harm and it seemed to her that it was a direct sign from heaven that she should look for other work . . . To strengthen this argument, it was her half-day; usually spent in cleaning the house.

She got home about two o'clock and, instead of getting into an apron and getting out the vacuum cleaner, she went to her room, put on a clean blouse, brushed her blue skirt, did her hair in a severe style which did nothing for her looks, and went downstairs.

'Why are you going out?' enquired her father suspiciously.

'Don't worry, Father, I'll be back to get you your tea.' She skipped through the door before he could answer.

It was barely five minutes' walk to the Wheel House and Florina didn't give herself time to get nervous. She thumped the knocker, firmly, and then took several deep breaths. She had read somewhere that deep breathing helped if one felt nervous.

The door was opened and there was a tall, bony woman with grey hair and faded blue eyes. She looked stern and rather unwelcoming, so that Florina was glad of the deep breaths.

'Good afternoon. Mrs Datchett told me this morning that you were wanting a cook...'

'Sir William is wanting a cook. I'm the housekeeper. Do come in.'

She was led into a small sitting-room in the kitchen wing. 'Why do you want to come?'

'I work at a hotel in Wilton—I've been there for several years. I cycle there and back each day. I'd like to work on my own.' Florina added, anxiously, 'I'm a good cook, I can get references.'

'You live here?'

'Yes, just this side of the bridge.'

'You'd have to be here by eight o'clock each morning, make out the menus, keep the kitchen clean, cook lunch if Sir William is here, and dinner as well. You'd be free in the afternoons. You'd have help with the washing up and so on, but you might have to stay late some evenings. Do you want to live in?'

'I live very close by and I have to look after my father...'

The housekeeper nodded. 'Well, you're not quite what I had in mind, but I dare say you'll suit. You can come on a month's trial. There's Sir William at weekends, his daughter, Pauline, living here with me, and you must be prepared to cook for guests at the weekends. You do know that Sir William intends to marry?'

Florina shook her head. She hadn't realised until that moment that Sir William loomed so large in her life. The idea of him marrying left her with a feeling of disquiet, but she had no time to wonder about it, for the housekeeper said, 'Sir William will be moving in at the end of next week. Can you start then? A month's trial and, mind, he expects the best.'

She had to give a week's notice. She would go and see the hotel manager in the morning, for that would give him ten days in which to find someone to take her place.

'You haven't asked what your wages will be,' said the housekeeper, and mentioned a sum which sent Florina's ginger eyebrows up.

'That's a good deal more than I'm getting now,' she pointed out.

'Probably, but you'll have to work for it.'

'I'd like to work here,' said Florina. She would see Sir William sometimes, even if he never spoke to her.

'Very well, you'll get a letter in a day or two. My name is Frobisher, Miss Martha Frobisher. If you have any problems you'll bring them to me. Sir William is a busy man, he hasn't the time to bother with household matters.' She eyed Florina's small, neat person. 'What is your name?'

'Payne—Florina Payne.'

They wished each other goodbye with guarded politeness.

Mr Payne, apprised of his daughter's astonishing behaviour, called upon heaven to defend him from ungrateful daughters, painted a pathetic picture of his early death from neglect and starvation, since there would be no one to look after him. Finally he declared that he might as well be dead.

'Nonsense, Father,' said Florina kindly. 'You know that's not true. I'm likely to be at home more than I am now. You've had to boil your kettle for breakfast for years now, and I'll leave your lunch ready just as usual...'

'The housework—the whole place will go to rack and ruin.'

'I shall be home each afternoon, I can do the chores then. Besides, the doctor said it would do you good to be more active now you're better.'

'I shall never be better...'

Florina said cheerfully, 'I'll make a cup of tea. You'll feel better then.'

The manager was sorry that she wished to leave, but he understood that the chance of a job so close to her home wasn't to be missed. He wrote out a splendid reference which she slid through the letter-box at Wheel House, together with her letter accepting the job. If she didn't suit, of course, it would mean that she would be out of work at the end of a month; but she refused to entertain that idea, for she knew she was a good cook.

She went to the Wheel House the day before she was to start work, so that she might have a good look round her kitchen. It had everything, and the pantry and cupboards and fridge were bulging with food. She spent a satisfying afternoon arranging everything to her liking, and then went home to get her father's tea, a meal she sat through while he grumbled and complained at her lack of filial devotion. It was a relief, once she had tidied their meal away, to walk back to Wheel House and put the finishing touches to the kitchen. Miss Frobisher was upstairs somewhere, and the old house was quiet but for the gentle sound of running water from the mill. She had left the kitchen door open so the setting sun poured in, lighting the whole place as she made the last of her preparations for thc morning. Sir William and Paulinc would bc arriving after lunch; she would bake a cake and scones in the morning and prepare everything for dinner that evening. She would have all day, so she wouldn't need to hurry.

She crossed to the door to close it and, with a final look round, went down the passage to the front hall. Sir William was standing there, his hands in his pockets, his head on one side, contemplating a large oil painting of a prissy-looking young lady in rose-coloured taffeta and ringlets, leaning over a gilded chair.

He glanced over his shoulder at her. 'Hello. She doesn't seem quite right there, does she? One of my more strait-laced forebears.' He smiled. 'I expect you're here for some reason?'

At the sight of him, Florina was experiencing a variety of sensations: a sudden rush of delight, peevishness at the thought of her untidy appearance, a deep sadness that he hadn't a clue as to who she was, which of course was ridiculous of her. And woven through this a variety of thoughts . . . suitable food which could be cooked quickly if he needed a meal.

He was watching her with faint amusement. 'Have we met?' He snapped a finger. 'Of course! You were so good as to tell us where we might stay when we first came here.'

'Yes,' said Florina breathlessly, 'that's me. I'm the cook. Miss Frobisher engaged me, but only if you approve.' She added to make it quite clear, 'I'm on a month's trial.'

'You don't look much like a cook.' He stared rather hard at the ginger plait hanging over one shoulder. 'But the proof of the pudding . . . as they say.'

He turned round as Miss Frobisher bustled in. 'Nanny, how nice to see you. I'm here a day too soon, aren't I? I've left Pauline with her aunt, but I'll drive back tomorrow and fetch her after lunch. I had a consultation in Salisbury and it seemed a good idea to come on here instead of driving back to town. Is everything just as it should be?'

'Aye, Sir William, it is. You'll be tired, no doubt. Cook will get you a light meal . . .'

'No need. I'll go to the Trout and Feathers. And I can't call you "cook", not with that pigtail. What is your name?'

'Florina Payne.' She caught Mrs Frobisher's stern eye, and added, 'Sir William.'

'Not an English name, but a pretty one.'

'My mother was Dutch, sir.'

'Indeed! I go to Holland from time to time.' He added kindly, 'Well, Florina, we'll see you in the morning—or do you live in?'

'In the village.'

'I'll need to leave early,' he observed, and strolled away towards the drawing-room.

Mrs Frobisher said, in a warning voice, 'So you had best be here at half-past seven, Florina, for he will want his breakfast at eight o'clock. You can have your own breakfast with me after he has gone.'

Florina glanced at the broad back disappearing through the open door of the drawing-room. She found the idea of cooking his breakfast positively exciting; an idea, she told herself sternly, which was both pointless and silly.

All the same, the thought of it sustained her through her father's diatribe when she got back home.

She made tea before she left in the morning, and took a cup up to her father, bade him a cheerful good morning, reminded him that everything was ready for his breakfast, just as usual, and walked quickly through the still quiet village. Wheel House was quiet, too. She went in through the kitchen door, using the key Mrs Frobisher had given her, and set to work. The kettle was boiling and the teapot warming when Sir William wandered in, wrapped in a rather splendid dressing-gown. She turned from cutting bread for toast and wished him a polite good morning. 'Where would you like your tea, sir?' she asked him. 'Breakfast will be in half an hour, sooner, if you wish.'

'Half an hour is fine. And I'll have my tea here.' He fetched a mug from the dresser, poured his tea and went to stand in the open doorway. 'What's for breakfast?'

'Bacon and eggs, with mushrooms, fried bread and tomato. Then, toast and marmalade, tea or coffee, sir.'

'Where did you learn to cook?' he asked idly.

'My mother taught me and I took a cookery course in Salisbury. I worked at the hotel in Wilton for several years.'

He nodded. 'I shall have guests sometimes. You could cope with that?'

She said seriously, 'Oh, yes.' She put a frying pan on the Aga. 'Would you like more tea, sir?'

He shook his head. 'Why not have a cup yourself?' He wandered to the door. 'Pauline will be glad to see you—she'll be here this afternoon.'

She set the table in the dining-room, and was making the toast when Miss Frobisher came into the kitchen. She eyed the laden tray with approval and her greeting held more warmth than usual. 'Sir William always likes a good breakfast; he's a big man and needs his strength for his work.' She shot a look at Florina. 'He's a doctor, did you know that? A very well known one. He was a dear little boy, I always knew he'd be successful. You'd better take that tray in, I can hear him coming downstairs.'

Florina laid the food on the table before him, casting a motherly glance at him hidden behind the morning paper. She had liked him on sight, she remembered, and that liking was growing by the minute. She would very much like to know all about him, of course, though she had the good sense to know that she never would.

CHAPTER TWO

THERE was plenty to keep Florina busy that morning. After breakfast, shared with Mrs Frobisher, there was the menu to put together, the cake and scones to make and everything to prepare for the evening. That done, there was coffee to make for Mrs Frobisher, Mrs Deakin and Mrs Datchett, who came to sit around the kitchen table for a short break from their polishing and dusting. The latter two ladies were inclined to gossip, but received short shrift from the housekeeper, who didn't answer their questions about the new owner and silenced them with an intimidating eye.

'But he is going to marry?' persisted Mrs Deakin, not easily put off.

'It seems very likely,' conceded Mrs Frobisher, and Florina thought that there was a trace of disquiet in the housekeeper's voice.

Florina left an excellent light lunch ready for the housekeeper, and took herself off home to get a meal for her father and herself. The breakfast dishes were still on the table and he was sitting in a chair, reading the paper.

He greeted her with a disgruntled, 'So there you are, and high time too!' Then he picked up his paper again, leaving her to clear the table, wash up and get a snack meal.

They ate in silence and Florina made short work of tidying everything away. Cleaning the house, dusting and carpet-sweeping took her another half an hour; there was an hour of leisure before she needed to return to Wheel House. She spent it in the big garden behind the cottage, weeding and tying back the clumps of old-fashioned flowers her mother had planted years ago, and which Florina tended still. She made tea for her father before she went, drank a cup herself, tidied her already neat person and returned to Wheel House. She had left everything ready for tea, and as she went round the back of the house to the kitchen wing she could hear the little girl's excited voice from the drawing-room, the door of which was open as she passed. Her hand was on the kitchen door when she was stopped.

The girl rushed at her from the room. 'I'm Pauline—oh, isn't this fun? Have you seen my room? It's pink and white! We've eaten almost all the scones and half the cake. Daddy says you must be a treasure in the kitchen.'

'Hello,' said Florina, and beamed at the pretty little face grinning at her. 'I'm so glad you enjoyed the cake. I'm going to get dinner ready now.'

'I'll help you.'

Pauline danced into the kitchen, examining the pots and saucepans, opening the cupboards and peering inside, peeping into the fridge. Florina, changing out of her dress into the striped cotton frock and large white apron which was her uniform while she was working, called from the little cloakroom leading from the kitchen, 'Put everything back where you found it, won't you, Pauline?'

She reappeared to collect the ingredients for the watercress soup, *boeuf en croûte*, and the chocolate sauce to go with the profiteroles.

Florina worked steadily, undeterred by Pauline's stream of excited chatter. She was chopping mint and

Pauline was sitting on the table, running a finger round the remnants of the chocolate sauce in the pan, when Sir William wandered in.

'Something smells delightful. Is it a secret?'

'Watercress soup, *boeuf en croûte*, potatoes with mint, courgettes, new carrots, spinach purée, profiteroles with chocolate sauce, cheese and biscuits and coffee,' recited Florina, finishing the last of the sauce.

'It sounds good. Are you cordon bleu trained, Florina?'

'Yes, but I think I learnt almost everything from my mother—the cordon bleu just—just put the polish on.'

She had washed her hands, and was piling profiteroles into a pyramid on a china dish. It crossed her mind that she felt completely at ease with Sir William, as though she had known him for years . . . She really must remember to call him Sir William. 'Dinner will be at half-past seven unless you would like to change that, Sir William?'

He said carelessly, 'Oh, no, why should I change it? I'll take Pauline off your hands—we'll go for a stroll.'

Without Pauline's pleasant chatter and her father's large presence, the kitchen seemed empty and quiet. Florina went to and fro, putting the finishing touches to the food. She was a little warm by now, but still very neat. Mrs Frobisher, coming into the kitchen, nodded approvingly.

'You certainly know your work,' she allowed. 'Sir William is a very punctual man, so have the soup ready on the dot. I'll carry in the food.'

The meal over and the last of the dishes back in the kitchen, Florina put the coffee tray ready to be carried in, and started on the clearing up.

The china, glass and silver Mrs Deakin would see to in the morning, but she did her saucepans and cooking utensils. It had been a strict rule at the hotel and one she intended to continue. She had just finished burnishing the last pan when Mrs Frobisher came back with the coffee tray. 'Sir William is very satisfied with your cooking,' she told Florina, 'I'm to pass on his compliments. He wants to know if you can cook for a dinner party next weekend. Eight sitting down to table, and Miss Fortesque, his fiancée, will be staying for the weekend.'

'No problem. If there is anything special Sir William wants, I'll do my best.'

'I'll ask him. You're finished? Did you put everything to keep warm in the Aga? Good. I'll lay the table and you dish up. It's been a busy evening, but you've done very well. I've suggested to Sir William that we get a girl from the village to come in in the evenings and help you clear up and see to the vegetables and so on. Do you know of one?'

Florina thought. 'Yes, there is Jean Smith at Keeper's Cottage—she's left school, but she's got to wait a month or two before she can start work training as a nurse. She will be glad of the money.'

'I'll leave you to ask her to come along and see me. Now, let's have dinner. I've seen Pauline safely up to bed, and Sir William has got all he wants. Your father knows you won't be home until later?'

'Oh, yes. I left his supper ready for him.'

'You're kept busy,' observed Mrs Frobisher. 'Mind you, during the week it will be midday dinner and a light supper at seven o'clock. You'll have most of the evening free. It is a pity that you can't live in.'

'Oh, I don't mind working late or coming early in the morning,' said Florina, and tried not to sound anxious.

She did not quite succeed, though, for Mrs Frobisher said quickly, 'Oh, don't worry about that dinner, Sir William won't want to lose you on any account. I was only thinking that it would be much easier for you; there's a nice little room at the top of the back stairs with its own bathroom, and nicely furnished, too. Still, I dare say your father would miss you.'

Florina, serving them with the last of the profiteroles, agreed quietly.

She faced a long-drawn-out lecture when she got home. She listened with half an ear while she washed up his supper things and put everything ready for the morning. When her father paused at last, she surprised him and herself by saying, without heat, 'Father, the doctor said that it would be good for you to do a few things for yourself. There's no reason why you shouldn't clear away your meals and wash up. You could make your bed, too, and get your own tea. I'm really working hard for most of the day, and I give you almost all my money. You could even get a part-time job! Then you would have more money and I could have some money of my own.'

She waited patiently while he gobbled and snorted, and told her several times that she was a wicked and ungrateful girl.

'Why?' asked Florina. 'It's not wicked to get you to help a little, especially when the doctor says it would be good for you. And what do I have to be grateful for, Father?'

'A roof over your head, and food and a bed!' he shouted very angrily.

She could get those if she lived in at Wheel House... 'I'm thinking of leaving home,' she told him. 'I'll stay until you can get someone to come in and keep the house tidy and do the washing. You said a few days ago that a cousin of yours—Aunt Meg, was it? I don't remember her very well—had been widowed. She might be glad to come and live here with you...'

'You would leave your home? But you were born here, your mother lived here.'

'Yes, I know, Father, but now she isn't here any more it isn't home, not to me.' She added gently, 'You'll be happier if I'm not here, won't you?'

Her father's face turned alarmingly red. 'To think that a daughter of mine should say such a thing...'

'But it's true, isn't it, Father? And if Aunt Meg were here, she would be at home all day and be company for you. You wouldn't miss my money because she would pay her share, wouldn't she?'

He agreed in a grumbling voice. 'And, since you are determined to leave home and leave me to shift for myself, I'll write to her, I suppose. But don't you think you can come sneaking back here if you're ever out of a job.'

'There is always work for a good cook,' observed Florina.

Sunday was very much like Saturday, except that there was hot lunch and cold supper, which gave Florina a good deal more leisure. She left everything ready for tea and, intent on striking while the iron was hot, asked Mrs Frobisher if she had been serious when she had suggested that for her to live in would be more convenient for everyone.

'Yes, of course I was,' declared that lady. 'Why do you ask?'

Florina explained, leaving out the bits about her father's bad temper.

'A good idea. Come and see the room.'

It was a very nice room, its windows overlooking the river running through the garden. It was well furnished, too, with a small writing desk and an easy chair with a table beside it, and a divan bed along one wall with a fitted cover. There were pictures on the walls and a window-box cascading geraniums. There was a cupboard in one wall and a small bathroom, cunningly built into the roof. A minuscule kitchen contained a sink and a minature gas cooker, capable of turning out a meal for one, as well as an electric kettle.

'Why, it's perfect! Whoever thought of it?'

'Sir William. He enjoys comfort, and wants everyone around him to be comfortable, too. I believe that he will be pleased if you were to live here, Florina, but of course I'll say nothing until you've decided.'

She had a good deal more leisure for the rest of the week. Sir William left early on the Monday morning, but that leisure was very much encroached on by Pauline, who attached herself to Florina at every possible moment. Though Florina, who had perforce led a somewhat solitary life, enjoyed her company; it was fun to show the child where she could find mushrooms and wild strawberries, sit by the river and watch for water voles, and feed the swans. Pauline, who had spent almost all her life in London, loved every minute of it. But, if life was pleasant while she was at the Wheel House, it was uncomfortable at home. Her father had indeed written to her aunt, and received a reply, full of enthusiasm for his scheme and suggesting that she would be ready to join him in a couple of weeks' time, news which apparently gave him no pleasure at all. Not that he wanted Florina to change her plans. Indeed, she had told him Mrs Frobisher knew that she was willing to live in, providing Sir William agreed. Cutting sandwiches for Pauline's tea, she had never felt so happy.

It had to be too good to last. On Friday morning she began her preparations for the weekend. She and Mrs Frobisher had decided on a menu, and the housekeeper had gone to Wilton and bought everything for Florina on her list, so it had only remained for her to assemble them ready for Saturday evening. Mrs Frobisher, who seemed to like her, in a guarded manner, had taken her upstairs in the afternoon to show her the guest room.

'Miss Fortesque is used to town ways,' she explained. 'She'll expect her breakfast in bed...' She sniffed. 'She'll not want me here when they're married.'

'But were you not Pauline's Nanny?'

'And Sir William's before her.' Miss Fortesque forgotten momentarily, Mrs Frobisher threw open the two doors close to the room they were viewing. 'Guest rooms,' she pointed out. 'Pauline's room is on the other side of the landing, as is Sir William's. You've noticed that there are more rooms above the kitchen. The housekeeper's—I sleep on this landing at present because otherwise Pauline would be alone... There is another bathroom and a third bedroom. I dare say Miss Fortesque will want someone else to live in. It's a large house and I doubt if she knows what a duster looks like.'

Certainly, dusters were the last things one would think of at the sight of Miss Fortesque, thought Florina, watching from the kitchen window as she stepped from Sir William's car on Saturday morning.

She was the picture of elegance, the sort of elegance never seen in the village: a sleeveless dress of what Florina was sure was pure silk in palest blue, Italian sandals and enormous hoop ear-rings matching the gold bracelets on her arms. Florina sighed without knowing it, twitched her apron so that it covered her small person correctly, and went back to the preparation of *crêpes de volaille Florentine*. She was making the cheese sauce when Sir William wandered into the kitchen.

'Hello,' he said. 'Every time I see you, you're slaving over a hot stove.'

She couldn't prevent her delight at seeing him showing on her face, although she didn't know that. 'I'm the cook, sir,' she reminded him.

'Yes—I seem to have difficulty in remembering that.' He smiled at her and called over his shoulder, 'Wanda, come and meet Florina.'

Miss Fortesque strolled in and linked an arm in his. 'Oh, hello. You're the cook?'

The air positively hummed with their mutual dislike, instantly recognized, even if silent. Sir William watched them from half-shut lids.

'Florina is our treasure—she cooks like a dream, and Pauline considers her to be her best friend.'

Wanda opened large blue eyes. 'Oh, the poor child, has she no friends of her own sort?' She made a small gesture. 'Is it wise to let her live here, William? At a good boarding-school she would make friends with all the right children.'

'Who are the right children?' he asked carelessly. 'Don't be a snob, Wanda. Pauline is happy; she'll be going to day school in Wilton in September, and there's plenty to occupy her here meantime.' He glanced at Florina. 'Does she bother you, Florina?'

'Not in the least, Sir William. She is learning to cook and she spends a great deal of time gardening. She and Mrs Frobisher go for long walks.'

Miss Fortesque turned on her heel. 'Oh, well, if you're quite content to leave her with the servants . . .' She smiled bewitchingly, 'I shall alter all that, of course. When are the others arriving?'

Florina was left to seethe over the Aga. The horrible girl was quite unsuitable to be Sir William's wife, and she would be a disastrous stepmother. If Sir William was as easy-going as he appeared to be, then Pauline would find herself at a boarding-school, and she and Nanny would be out of jobs. Not too bad for Nanny, for she had already officially retired, but it would mean finding work for herself, and away from home, too.

Despite her rage, she served up a lunch which was perfection itself, and shared a quick meal with Nanny. When Sir William, with his fiancée and Pauline, had driven off for a brief tour of the surrounding country, Florina arranged the tea tray and then got down to preparing dinner. The house was quiet: Mrs Frobisher had gone to put her feet up before tea, Mrs Deakin was doing the last of the washing up and Florina concentrated on her cooking. By the time she heard the car stop by the house, she was satisfied that there was nothing more to do for an hour or so.

Two other cars arrived then, and Mrs Frobisher, much refreshed by the nap, carried in the tea tray and the assortment of cakes and sandwiches Florina had got ready, before she came back to share a pot of tea with Florina.

The kitchen was warm; she opened the windows wide and sat down gratefully, listening to Mrs Frobisher describing Sir William's guests. Rather nice, she was told, and had known him for years—doctors and their wives, rather older than he was.

'And, of course, Miss Fortesque,' added Nanny, and she sounded as though she had inadvertently sucked on a lemon. 'A well preserved woman, one might say, but of course she spends a great deal of time and money upon herself.'

Obviously Nanny didn't approve of Sir William's Wanda, but Florina didn't dare to say so; she murmured vaguely and her companion went on, 'Had her claws into him for months. I'm surprised at him—she'll be a bad wife for him and a worse stepmother for my little Pauline.' She passed her cup for more tea. 'He's so busy with all those sick children, he only sees her when she's dressed up and all charm and prettiness. Of course, that's very nice for the gentlemen when they've had a hard day's work, but when all's said and done they want a wife as well, someone who'll sit on the opposite side of the fireplace and knit while he reads the papers, listen when he wants to talk, and love his children.' Nanny snorted. 'All she likes to do is dance and play bridge.'

'Perhaps she'll change,' suggested Florina gently, not quite sure if she should voice an opinion. Nanny was obviously labouring under strong feelings, and possibly she would regret her outburst later on.

'You're a good girl,' said Nanny, 'I've wanted to say all that to someone for weeks, and you're the only person I've felt I could talk to.'

To Florina's distress, Mrs Frobisher's eyes filled with tears. 'I had him as a baby,' she said.

'They're not married yet,' ventured Florina. She added, very thoughtfully, 'It just needs someone to give fate a push and change things . . .'

Mrs Frobisher blew her nose, an awesome sound. 'You're a sensible girl as well as a good one, Florina.'

Florina dished up a splendid dinner: artichoke hearts with a sharp dressing of her own invention, lobster cardinal, medallions of beef with a wine sauce and truffles, and tiny pancakes filled with strawberries and smothered in thick cream.

When the coffee tray had gone in, she and Nanny sat down to eat what was left, before Nanny went away to see Pauline into bed. Mrs Deakin had come back to help with the clearing up, but all the same the evening was far gone, and Sir William seeing his guests on their way, by the time they were finished in the kitchen. Florina set everything ready for the morning, changed into her dress and, with Mrs Deakin for company, locked the kitchen door after her and started for home.

They were at the gate when Sir William loomed out from the shrubs alongside the short drive. 'A delightful meal, Florina! My compliments, and thank you, and Mrs Deakin, for working late.'

Mrs Deakin muttered happily; she was being paid overtime, and generously, for any work she did over and above her normal hours. Florina said quietly, 'Thank you, Sir William. Goodnight.'

He would go into his lovely house presently, she supposed, and Wanda would be waiting for him. Florina had caught a glimpse of her during the evening—a vision in scarlet chiffon. Enough to turn any man's head, even that of the placid, good-natured Sir William.

She was making a salad the next day when Miss Fortesque, in a startling blue jersey dress and a great many gold bangles, strolled into the kitchen.

'Hello, Cook, busy among your saucepans again? It's really surprising that even in the depths of the country it's possible to find someone who can turn out a decent meal.' She smiled sweetly. 'After town standards, you know, one hardly expects it.'

Florina shredded lettuce with hands which shook very slightly with temper, and said nothing.

'That sauce last night,' continued her visitor, 'I fancied that there was a touch too much garlic in it. Sir William didn't complain—he's really too easy-going...'

'When Sir William complains to me, Miss Fortesque, I shall listen to him,' said Florina very evenly.

Wanda's eyes opened wide. 'Don't you dare to speak to me like that, Cook! I'll have you dismissed...' She advanced, rather unwisely, too close to Florina, who had started to whip up a dressing for the salad. She increased her beating with a vigour which sent oily drops in all directions. The blue dress would never be the same again; a shower of little blobs had made a graceful pattern down its front.

Wanda's breath was a hiss of fury. 'You clumsy fool—look what you've done! It's ruined—I'll have to have a new dress, and I'll see that it's stopped out of your wages! I'll...'

Sir William's voice, very placid, cut her short. 'My dear Wanda, if you hadn't been standing so close, it wouldn't have happened. You can't blame Florina, you've only yourself to thank. Surely you know that cooks must be left in peace in their kitchens when they are cooking?'

Wanda shot him a furious glance. She said pettishly, 'I'll have to go and change. I hope you'll give the girl a good telling-off.'

She flounced out of the kitchen and Florina began to slice tomatoes very thinly. Sir William spoke from the door. 'I found the sauce exactly right,' he said gently, and wandered away.

He took his fiancée back to town that evening, leaving behind a rather unhappy Pauline. He sought out Florina before he left, to tell her that for the next few weeks, while the child was on holiday, he would come down each weekend on Friday afternoons, and drive back early on Monday morning.

'Nanny tells me that you may decide to move in with us. Your father doesn't object to being alone?'

Her aunt had written to say that she would be arriving at the end of the week. She told him this, leaving out the details. He nodded pleasantly. 'I'm sure it will give you more leisure. I hope you'll be happy here. Pauline will be over the moon when you tell her.'

She thought wistfully that it would have been nice if he had expressed the same satisfaction, even if in a more modified form. She bade him a quiet good-night, more or less drowned by Miss Fortesque's voice, pitched high, demanding that they should leave at once.

The week unfolded at a leisurely pace; Florina packed her things, got her room ready for her aunt and moved to the Wheel House. Her father bade her goodbye with no sign of regret, merely warning her again that she need not expect to go crying back to him when she found herself out of a job. She received this remark without rancour, aware that if he should fall ill again the first thing that he would do would be to demand that she should return home to look after him.

She enjoyed arranging her few possessions in her room at Wheel House, helped by a delighted Pauline. Once settled in, she found that she had a good deal more leisure. Cooking for the three of them took up only a part of her day; she helped Nanny with the ironing and the cleaning of the silver, took Pauline mushrooming in the early mornings, and, with Mrs Frobisher's consent, started to give her cooking lessons. By the time Sir William arrived on Friday afternoon, there was a dish of jam tarts and a fruit cake, a little soggy in the middle but still edible, both of which Pauline bore to the tea table with pride. Sir William, a kind and loving parent, ate quantities of both.

The weekend was one of the happiest Florina had spent for a long time. For one thing, there was a peaceful content over the old home. Sir William insisted that they all breakfast together in the kitchen, a meal which Florina cooked with an almost painful wish to serve up something to perfection, just to please him. She succeeded very well; he ate everything put before him, carrying on a cheerful conversation meanwhile, even making Nanny laugh, something she seldom did. They were at the toast and marmalade stage on Saturday morning, when Pauline said, 'I wish it could be like this always—just us, Daddy—you and me and Nanny and Florina. Must you marry Wanda? She wouldn't sit at the kitchen table, and she's always fussing about eating in case she gets fat.'

Florina saw the look on Sir William's face. There was a nasty temper hidden away behind that calm exterior, and to avert it she got to her feet, exclaiming loudly, 'Shall I make another pot of coffee? And how about more toast?' At the same time she cast a warning glance at Pauline.

The child had gone very red and tears weren't far off. She sighed and said, 'I'm sorry, Daddy.'

His face was placid again. 'That's all right, darling. What are we going to do today?'

The pair of them went off presently, and Florina prepared lunch, decided what to have for dinner, made the coffee and went to help Nanny with the beds. The rest of the weekend was peaceful, and Florina, taking along the coffee tray to the patio where Sir William had settled with the Sunday papers after church, while Pauline fed the swans, thought how delightful life was.

She gave him breakfast the next morning, happily aware that he would be back on Friday afternoon. Wanda Fortesque had gone to stay with friends in the south of France, and Florina allowed herself the childish hope that something, anything, would prevent her from ever coming back from there!

The weather changed suddenly during the day, by the evening it was chilly and grey, and Pauline seemed to have the beginnings of a cold.

Nanny came down to the kitchen after she had seen Pauline to bed. 'The child's feverish,' she declared. 'I think I'd better keep her in bed tomorrow; these summer colds can be heavy.'

But when morning came, Pauline was feeling worse; moreover, she had a pinky, blotchy rash.

'Measles,' said Nanny, and phoned for the doctor.

He came from Wilton that morning, confirmed Nanny's diagnosis, and observed that there was a lot of it about and that Pauline, having had an anti-measles injection when she was a little girl, would soon be on her feet again. 'Plenty to drink,' he advised, 'and keep her in bed until her temperature is down.'

He patted Nanny reassuringly on the shoulder. 'Nothing to worry about.'

All the same, Nanny telephoned Sir William in London, only to be told that he was at the hospital and would be there all day. She put the phone down, undecided as to what to do, when it rang again.

Florina, making iced lemonade for the invalid, heard her talking at some length, and presently she came back to the kitchen.

'Sir William's not at home and won't be until the evening, but Miss Fortesque was there. She rang back when I told her I wanted him urgently, said she would tell him when he got back. I would rather have phoned the hospital, but that would be no use if he is in the theatre or the out-patients.'

By the time they were ready for bed, more than ready, for Florina had suggested that neither Mrs Deakin nor Mrs Datchett came to work until Pauline was better, for they both had children, there had been no word from Sir William. Nanny telephoned once more, only to be told by Miss Fortesque that he was still out.

Pauline was much better in the morning and Nanny, while still a tiny bit puzzled as to why Sir William hadn't telephoned, decided that there was no need to bother him, not until the evening at any rate. She and Florina spent another busy day, for the house was large and there was a certain amount of work to get through, as well as pandering to Pauline's increasing whims. Nanny had a headache by teatime, and Florina persuaded her to go to bed early.

'Only if you telephone Sir William,' declared Nanny.

Florina waited until she had taken up two supper trays, eaten a scratch meal of beans on toast herself, before dialling the number she had been given. Miss Fortesque answered. No, Sir William wasn't at home and wasn't likely to be for some time and was it urgent? He had had a busy day and needed his rest. She slammed down the receiver before Florina had got her mouth open.

Nanny had a rash in the morning, a high temperature, a terrible headache and a firmly rooted opinion that she was going to die.

'Nonsense, Mrs Frobisher,' said Florina robustly. 'You've got the measles. I'm going to get the doctor.'

He wasn't quite as cheerful about Nanny. It transpired that she had never had measles as a child, an illness, which he pointed out to Florina, that could be quite serious in anyone as elderly as Nanny. 'Keep her in bed,' he advised. 'Plenty of fluids, and don't let her read or use her eyes. Keep the blinds drawn and take her temperature every four hours. I'll be out to see her again tomorrow.' He added as an afterthought, 'Can you manage?'

Sir William would be home on the next day, so Florina assured the doctor that, of course, she could manage.

It was hard work. Pauline had made a quick recovery, although she still needed looking after and had to stay in bed for another day or so, but Nanny, suddenly an old, ill Nanny, needed constant attention. Not that she was a difficult patient, but she was feverish, her head ached and she fretted at lying in bed.

Florina, trotting up and down stairs with trays and cool drinks, was tempted to telephone Sir William again, but it hardly seemed worth it since he would be home in less than twenty-four hours. She settled her two patients for the night at last, and went to the kitchen to make out a menu for Sir William's dinner for the following evening. It would have to be something quick, and which could be left in the Aga to look after itself. She made a chocolate mousse and put it in the freezer, made a vegetable soup, and then decided that she would make a cheese soufflé—something which could be done at the last minute. She had picked some peas and beans earlier in the day, and there was plenty of fruit and cheese and biscuits. She went to take a last look at her two patients and then went to bed herself, to sleep the moment her head touched the pillow.

Doctor Stone came again the next morning, cautioned her that Pauline should stay in bed for another day or so, declared that Nanny was holding her own nicely, but that she would need careful nursing, accepted a cup of coffee and remarked that Florina was managing very well.

'No need to send you a nurse,' he told her, 'and, since there isn't one available at the moment, that's a good thing. Is Sir William coming down for the weekend?'

Florina said that, yes, he was, and thought tiredly of all the extra cooking there would be. She was, after all, the cook, and he had every right to expect well prepared meals to be set before him. Doctor Stone went, and she made a large quantity of lemonade, then made herself a sandwich and started to get a light lunch for Pauline. Nanny didn't want anything, but Florina made an egg nog and spent some precious time persuading her to drink it.

She spent more time settling Pauline for the afternoon. There was the radio, of course, and her cassette player, and since reading wasn't to be encouraged, a sketch-book had to be found with coloured crayons.

Florina, finally free to go to the kitchen, put on a clean apron, tossed her plait over her shoulder and started to shell the peas.

She was very tired; she let the sound of the stream, racing under the house and on into the garden, soothe her. She was disturbed five minutes later by a leisurely tread in the hall, and a moment later Sir William said from the kitchen door, 'Hello! The house is very quiet.'

When she turned to look at him he saw her white, tired face.

'What's wrong, Florina?'

She heard the sudden briskness of his usually placid voice. 'Measles,' she said. 'Pauline started on Monday and now Nanny has it... Yesterday—I've had the doctor. Doctor Stone, from Wilton.'

'Why wasn't I told?'

'Nanny telephoned you on Monday night, and then again on Tuesday. I rang again on Thursday evening...'

Sir William didn't answer. He went to the telephone on the wall by the Aga, and dialled a number. Florina went back to shelling her peas and listened.

'Jolly? Get hold of our Shirley and bribe her to sleep in for a few nights with Mrs Jolly. Then pack a bag and drive down here as soon as you can. Take the Rover and make all speed. We have a problem on our hands. Measles, no less!'

'On your own?' he asked, as he put back the receiver.

'Well, yes. You see, Mrs Deakin and Mrs Datchett have children.'

'Very wise. I'm going to take a look. Is Pauline on the mend? She had her jab when she was small.'

'Yes, she's over the worst. Mrs Frobisher is really quite ill, though...'

She heard him going upstairs two at a time.

By the time he returned she had finished the peas, had the kettle boiling for tea and had laid a tray with the tea things and a plate of scones.

He sat down at the kitchen table and told her to get another cup. 'Very spotty, the pair of them. Nanny's going to take a little while to get over it, but Pauline's well out of the wood.' He shot the next question at her so fast that she answered it without once pausing to think. 'Who answered the telephone when you and Nanny telephoned?'

'Miss Fortesque...' She went red because he would think her sneaky. 'I'm sure it was a misunderstanding...'

He didn't answer that. 'You've had your hands full—up for a good deal of the night, too?'

'Well, yes. Nanny felt so hot and ill, but Pauline slept well.'

His rather sleepy gaze swept round the kitchen. 'You've been running the place, and cooking, as well as looking after Pauline and Nanny?'

She misunderstood him completely. 'Oh, but I had all day. Dinner will be ready at half-past seven, but I can put it forward half an hour if you wish. I don't settle them for the night until about nine o'clock. Pauline likes her supper about eight o'clock and Nanny doesn't want to eat at present—I've been giving her egg and milk and tea and lemonade.'

He smiled at her suddenly. 'My poor dear, you are tired to the bone, aren't you? You've got dinner fixed already?' When she nodded, he continued, 'We'll eat here together, then you can get supper for Pauline and I'll take it up; I'll see that Nanny takes her fluids, too, and then I'll wash up while you get Pauline ready for bed.'

She opened her mouth to protest, but he lifted a large hand to stop her. 'I'm going back to take another look at Nanny and then to phone Doctor Stone. Which room should Jolly have when he comes?'

'There is the small guest room at the end of the passage where Nanny is—I'll make up the bed . . .'

'Put the bed linen out; I'll see to the bed, you stay here and get on with dinner.'

Florina, whose father had always considered the making of a bed to be a woman's work, was surprised, but Sir William had spoken in a voice which, while quiet, obviously expected to be obeyed. She cleared away the tea tray and set the kitchen table for the two of them before getting the ingredients for the soufflé.

Sir William was as good as his word; she was ready soon after seven o'clock, and he fetched the sherry decanter from the dining-room and poured each of them a glass, and then sat down opposite her and ate dinner with a splendid appetite, talking about nothing much. When they had finished, he sent her upstairs to Pauline. 'I'll fetch the tray down; you tidy her up for the night and then come back here.'

It was pleasant to have someone there to arrange things; Florina did as she was told and half an hour later went back downstairs to find Sir William, one of Nanny's aprons strained around his person, making the coffee.

'Sit down and drink it,' he ordered her, 'then, if you'll see to Nanny, I'll finish up down here and say goodnight to Pauline.'

Nanny was quite willing to be settled for the night. Everything, she told Florina, would be quite all right now that Sir William was home. 'You cooked him a good dinner?' she demanded.

Florina said that yes, she had, but she didn't mention that she had shared it with him at the kitchen table. There was no sense in sending Nanny's temperature up! She wished her goodnight and went yawning down the staircase; bed would be delightful, but first she must make sure that the kitchen was ready for the morning. Sir William would want his breakfast, and there was early-morning tea, and what about Jolly—who was Jolly, anyway?

The kitchen door to the garden was still open and Sir William was out on the patio, leaning over the balustrade, watching the stream below him.

'Come and have five minutes' peace,' he advised and she went to stand beside him, hot and dishevelled and very tired. He glanced sideways at her smiling faintly, surprised that it worried him to see her looking so weary. He didn't say anything and she was glad just to lean there, doing nothing until a car turning into the gates roused her.

'That will be Jolly,' said Sir William, and went round the side of the house to meet him.

CHAPTER THREE

FLORINA was still standing on the patio when Sir William returned, with Jolly beside him. Jolly was the antithesis of his name. He had a long, narrow face, very solemn and pale, dark eyes, and hair greying at the temples, smoothed to a satin finish. He was dressed soberly in a black jacket and striped trousers, and wore an old-fashioned wing-collar and a black bow-tie.

Sir William halted in front of Florina. 'This is Jolly, who runs my home. Jolly, this is Florina, who cooks for me and has been coping on her own for the last couple of days. I think we'll send her to bed and we'll discuss what's best to be done. Off you go, Florina, sleep the clock round if you want to.'

She was quite shocked. 'Breakfast . . .'

'Ah, you don't really trust us with the frying-pan. I dare say you're right. Breakfast is at half-past eight. You do the cooking, we'll clear up. We'll work out a routine in the morning. Now, off with you.'

It was difficult to go against this casual friendliness. Besides, she had had a long day. She said good-night to them both, and went upstairs to lie in the bath, half-asleep, and think about how nice Sir William was. But the cooling water brought her wide awake, and she tumbled into bed, to sleep soundly almost at once.

She was wakened by Sir William's voice, and shot up in bed, in an instant panic that she had overslept. He was wearing a rather grand dressing-gown, and stood by the bed with a mug from the kitchen in his hand.

He gave it to her and said cheerfully, 'Tea—you've slept well?' Then he sat himself down carefully on the side of the bed. He hadn't appeared to look at her, but he had taken in her face, rosy from sleep, her hair freed from its tidy plait, hanging in a mousy tangle round her shoulders. She looked a different girl from the pale, tired little creature he had found in the kitchen on the previous evening.

He went on easily, 'I've taken a look at our two invalids. Pauline is doing fine; Nanny's still feverish—she'll need a few days' nursing still, but luckily she's decided not to die this time, and is already giving orders about cleaning the bath and getting extra milk. A good sign!' He got off the bed. 'It's half-past seven. When you're ready, would you go along and make Nanny comfortable before breakfast? Jolly will see to the table for you and lay the trays and so forth. We'll eat in the kitchen; that will save dusting the dining-room.'

He smiled and nodded and wandered away, leaving her to drink her tea and then, as quickly as she could, to shower and dress, reflecting as she did so that she had never met anybody quite like him before. She couldn't remember her father ever bringing her a cup of tea in bed; he had always been at pains to point out to her, and her mother while she had been alive, that since a man spent his day working to keep a roof over their heads, it was only right that he should be properly looked after in his own home.

Her hair once more neatly plaited, wearing one of her striped cotton dresses, she went along to visit Pauline first, sitting up in bed and feeling so much better that she demanded to be allowed up.

'Not until your father says so,' said Florina briskly. 'I dare say he'll come to see you when he's had breakfast. What would you like? Are you hungry?'

They settled on scrambled eggs and, as Florina skimmed to the door, intent on dealing with Nanny, Pauline called after her, 'You are nice, Florina—the nicest friend I've ever had. Daddy likes you, too.'

A remark which sent a pleasant glow through Florina's person. It was delightful to be liked and needed. She beamed at Nanny's cross face, coaxed her to have her face and hands washed, smoothed her bed and suggested a pot of tea and some thin bread and butter.

'If you insist,' said Nanny peevishly, 'though I don't say I'll eat it.'

Jolly was in the kitchen, laying the table. He bade her a dignified good morning, expressed the hope that she had slept well, and started to cut bread for toast. Florina busied herself with the frying-pan, bacon, mushrooms and a bowl of eggs. 'Yes, thank you, Mr Jolly...'

'Jolly, miss. I am Sir William's manservant.'

She turned to look at him. 'Well, I'm his cook. I think that's what you should call me...'

His severe expression broke into a brief smile. 'If you don't object, I prefer to call you miss.'

'Well, if you want to, as long as Sir William doesn't mind.'

'What am I objecting to?' He was a large, rather heavily built man, but he moved with speed and silence.

'Mr—that is, Jolly wishes to call me miss, and I'm the cook...' She looked up briefly from scrambling eggs.

Sir William took a slice of bread and buttered it and began to eat.

'You're not Missus, are you?' he asked with interest.

'Certainly not!'

'Engaged or walking out, or whatever?'

'No, Sir William. Would you both like bacon and eggs and mushrooms and tomatoes?'

'Speaking for myself, yes, please, and I'm pretty sure Jolly would, too. Mrs Jolly always gives me fried bread and I dare say she gives it to Jolly, too.'

'Very well, Sir William. I'll just run up with Pauline's tray.'

'Give it to Jolly—what is Nanny having? Is this her tray? I'll take it up when you're ready.' He made the tea, whistling cheerfully, and presently they sat down to breakfast, a pleasant meal, with Sir William carrying on an easy conversation and Jolly, rather surprisingly, contributing his share of the talk. As for Florina, she had little to say. She was shy, for a start, and for another thing, meals with her father had been strictly for eating; no attempt had been made to enliven them with conversation.

Sir William got out the vacuum cleaner after breakfast and, while Jolly cleared the table and washed the dishes, he strode around his house, taking no notice of Florina's attempts to stop him, hoovering like a whirlwind.

'You have a poor opinion of my capabilities,' he observed. 'I think you should go away and shake up pillows and make beds. You can tell Pauline that if she stays quietly in bed, she may come down for tea this afternoon.'

She was half-way up the stairs when he asked, 'What are we eating for our lunch?' He switched off for a moment so that she could hear him. 'Ploughman's lunch? Then you won't need to cook. Is there any Stilton in the house?'

'Of course,' She spoke coldly, affronted that he should doubt her housekeeping.

He didn't notice. 'Good. Do you want any shopping done? I can run into Wilton with the car...' He was at the bottom of the staircase, looking up at her. 'Let me know when you come down.'

While she made the beds and attended to Pauline and Nanny, she reviewed the contents of the fridge and freezer. She would need eggs from the farm and a chicken as well as cream. There was a nice piece of beef in the freezer and vegetables in the garden. When she went back to the kitchen later, it was to find Jolly setting out mugs for coffee and bending in a dignified manner over the coffee-pot on the Aga. Smiling widely at him, despite his forbidding appearance, she felt sure he was a very reliable man and, in his reserved way, she felt also that he was disposed to like her. As for Sir William, she didn't allow herself to think too much about him; he resembled a little too closely for her peace of mind the rather vague dreams she had of the man who would sweep her off her feet and marry her and live with her happily ever after. She reminded herself once again that day-dreaming got you nowhere. Indeed, it was downright silly when you had your living to earn. She accepted a mug from Jolly, frowned fiercely when Sir William joined them, then she blushed, remembering how she had let her thoughts stray.

He gave her a quick glance and began to talk to Jolly. Presently, when he made some remark to her, she had regained her usual composed manner. The rest of the morning passed busily, and somehow the sight of Sir William standing at the sink scraping potatoes put her quite at her ease with him. The invalids attended to, the three of them sat down at the kitchen table again. She had made a bowl of salad, and Jolly had cut great hunks of bread and arranged the Stilton cheese on a dish flanked by pickles and chutney. Sir William had a tankard of beer beside him, Jolly had made himself a pot of tea and Florina had poured herself a glass of lemonade. Not at all the kind of meal Sir William was used to, reflected Florina, but he seemed happy enough, spreading his bread lavishly with butter and carving up the Stilton. They talked comfortably of small everyday matters and then fell to discussing how she should cook the chicken. '*Poulet au citron?*' suggested Florina, and caught Jolly's approving look.

'Nice,' observed Sir William, 'Mrs Jolly does a very nice *Poulet Normand*.'

This remark instantly put her on her mettle. 'If you prefer that, Sir William, I think I could manage it.'

He laughed. 'Don't be so modest, Florina. You could turn a stale loaf into a splendid meal with one hand tied behind your back!' He watched the colour wash over her cheeks; for a moment she looked quite pretty.

They were sitting at the table drinking their coffee, deciding which vegetables to have, when the front door was banged shut and high heels tapped across the hall's wooden floor. Wanda Fortesque pushed the kitchen door wide open and came to a halt just inside it, looking at them. It was evident that she was in a splendid rage and had no intention of hiding it, but Sir William didn't appear to have noticed that; he got up without haste.

'Wanda, my dear girl, what a delightful surprise!'

'Surprise?' she almost spat at him. 'I'd say it was a surprise! What's this? A *ménage à trois*?'

He said easily, 'Hardly, since there are five of us here. Come and sit down—have you lunched? Or would you like coffee?'

She stared at the table. 'I don't eat in the kitchen, William.' Her very beautiful lip curled. 'I thought you employed a cook.' Her peevish eye settled on Florina, sitting like a mouse, hardly daring to breathe. 'She can make me an omelette and salad and bring it to the dining-room. Oh, and some fruit. Why on earth is Jolly sitting here, doing nothing?'

Sir William put his hands in his pockets; he spoke pleasantly, but there was no expression on his face. 'Jolly is here because I asked him to come and, since you enquire, he has been working flat out since he arrived. You see, my dear, Nanny and Pauline have the measles—Nanny is quite ill. Florina had been managing on her own, deciding, quite rightly, that it was hardly fair to our usual help to expect them to come in from the village—measles is so very infectious . . .'

'Measles,' repeated Wanda, in a voice that had become a little shrill. She backed away. 'Why didn't you say so in the first place? I've not had them—the place must be full of germs.' She added wildly, 'It's spots, isn't it? Great red blotches, and puffy eyes and headaches.'

She turned on her heel and hurried back through the hall. Sir William went after her.

She turned to face him when they reached the door. 'Why didn't you tell me? You could have telephoned . . .' It was an accusation.

'I did,' he told her mildly. 'You weren't at home and you had left a message to say that I wasn't to ring you, you would ring me.' He added gently, 'I'm sorry you're upset, Wanda. Why not stay now you are here? You won't have to go near Pauline and Nanny.'

'You must be mad—supposing I caught them? There's the Springfields' party next week, and Mother is giving a dinner—and there is that dress show I simply mustn't miss . . .'

'Why not?' He was smiling now, but she didn't smile back.

'Don't be an idiot, William—I have to have clothes. I've hardly a rag to my back. I intend to be a wife you can be proud of. Besides, I know so many influential people; it's important to mix with the right people, especially when you're a doctor.'

He was still smiling but his eyes were chilly. 'I already mix with the right people, my dear. My patients.'

'You're impossible. I'll not listen to another word! You can come and apologise when you get back to town on Monday.'

He walked with her to her car. 'It doesn't seem likely that I'll be back on Monday,' he told her patiently, 'but I'll be in touch.'

Back in the kitchen he said calmly, 'Sorry about that—Miss Fortesque is rather—highly strung is the popular phrase, I believe. Some people are inordinately nervous of catching things.' He took the tea-towel from Florina and began to dry the dishes Jolly was washing.

'Will there be scones for tea?' he asked her. Then, as an afterthought, 'You've had measles?'

Florina said primly. 'No, but I don't in the least mind having them, though I'd rather not, as it would make things so awkward for everyone.'

He shouted with laughter and Jolly allowed himself a dry chuckle.

'Well, that's a bridge we'll cross when we come to it. What a boring job washing up is! Jolly, you should have told me...'

'It was mentioned a year or so ago, Sir William, if you remember, and a dishwasher was installed. A boon to Shirley, if I might say so.'

'Well, we'd better have one here, too. See to it, will you, Jolly?'

Florina, assembling the ingredients for the scones, marvelled at the way some people lived. Shouldn't he have consulted Miss Fortesque first? On second thoughts, no.

She put the scones in the Aga and went to see how the invalids were getting on. Pauline was happy enough, as good as gold in bed, knowing that presently she would be going downstairs for her tea. Nanny, however, badly needed a great deal of attention. She was hot, she was thirsty, she wanted her bed remade, and who had banged the front door and wakened her from a refreshing nap?

Florina soothed her, sped downstairs to take the scones from the oven, refill the jug of lemonade, and skip back again. Half an hour later, Nanny washed and in a fresh nightie, her bed remade, her hair combed, and sitting up against her pillows sipping lemonade, felt well enough to tell Florina that she was a good girl with a kind heart and she, for her part, was delighted to hear that Miss Fortesque had taken herself off again.

'I cannot think what Sir William sees in the creature,' she declared, and Florina silently agreed. Although perhaps a lovely face, and clothes in the height of fashion and an air of knowing that one was never wrong, could be irresistible to a man. She went down to the kitchen and got tea ready before starting on the chicken.

They played Monopoly after tea, still at the kitchen table, and Florina and Sir William took it in turns to visit Nanny. In between times she saw to dinner. There was a pause while everyone watched her pour the brandy into a skillet and hold a lighted match over it. The flames soared as she tipped the pan from side to side and, when they had died down, she poured the delicious liquid into the bowl of cream and covered the chicken before popping it into a pan and putting a lid on it. There was time for her to make her fortune at Monopoly, which she did while it simmered. Jolly laid the table, and Sir William went down to the cellar to fetch the wine while she made the sauce, cooked the rice and fried the triangles of bread to arrange around the chicken. Pauline had coaxed her father to let her stay up for dinner, and she sat watching Florina as she trotted to and fro between the table and the Aga, peering into the pans holding the baby carrots, the garden peas and the courgettes. Sir William, strolling in with the bottles under his arms, paused to watch her, her hair a little shaken loose from its plait, her small nose shining, intent on her work. A pleasant enough nonentity, he had decided when he had first seen her, but he had been wrong; small, unassuming and nothing much to look at, she still merited a second look. She would make a good nurse, too. He toyed with the idea and then discarded it. She was far too good a cook; besides, Pauline had developed a great liking for her.

'It smells delicious,' he observed, and put the bottles in the fridge. 'If I pour you a glass of sherry, will it upset the cooking?'

Everything was eaten, and Jolly pronounced the chicken every bit as good as that his wife could cook, adding rather severely, 'Although, of course, miss, it wouldn't do to go and tell her so.'

'It shall remain a secret, Jolly,' Sir William had promised. He smiled across the table at Florina. 'Did you conjure the crème caramel out of the air?'

She answered him quite seriously. 'No, Sir William. I baked them in the oven, with the milk pudding for Mrs Frobisher.'

'All of which she ate. Now take yourself off for an hour, while Jolly and I clear up.' When she would have protested he added, 'You need some fresh air, and heaven knows, you've earned some leisure.'

'I'll take a little walk then. Thank you both for washing up. First, I'll make sure that they are all right upstairs.'

She whisked herself out of the kitchen before he could say anything.

It was a light, warm evening for it was full summer. She strolled away from the village, past the outlying cottages, sniffing at the air, fragrant with meadowsweet, dog roses and valerian. She was tired, but she had enjoyed her day, all except the bit when Wanda Fortesque had walked in. Sir William, she reflected, must love her very much to put up with such peevishness. Florina sat on a gate and debated with herself as to whether she would like to go on working as the cook at Wheel House once Sir William had married. Or if, indeed, Wanda would want her to stay. It seemed unlikely; they shared a mutual dislike. On the other hand, if she stayed, Pauline would have someone to talk to. She was a nice child, and Sir William loved her, but she didn't think Wanda would make a good stepmother. From what Pauline had told her, her father had taken her with him whenever he could, and made sure that she had had all the usual treats a child of her age might expect: the circus, the pantomime, museums, sailing, swimming. Florina couldn't see Wanda taking part in any of them.

She wandered back presently, and stopped just inside the gates to look at the house. It was beautiful in the twilight, and the sound of the stream was soothing. The drawing-room curtains hadn't been drawn, and she could see Sir William sitting in an easy chair, smoking his pipe and reading. Jolly came in while she stood there and said something to him, then went away again, and a moment later the kitchen light was switched on. She thought guiltily that she had been away long enough, and went round the side of the house through the patio, past the open drawing-room doors.

'Had a pleasant walk?' asked Sir William from his chair.

'Yes, thank you. Is there anything else you would like, Sir William?' When he said no, nothing, she said, 'Then I'll say goodnight.'

Jolly was in the kitchen, laying the table for breakfast, and she thanked him for his help and added, 'I'll take a look at Pauline and Mrs Frobisher. Can I do anything for you before I go to bed?' She added shyly, 'You've done so much since you came, I'm so grateful...'

Jolly smiled. 'It's been a pleasure, miss. Goodnight.'

Sir William and Jolly didn't leave until Monday evening. Watching the car turn out of the drive, Florina felt a pang of loneliness. Sunday had been a lovely day, with Pauline allowed up for a good deal of it, Nanny feeling better at last, and Sir William and Jolly dealing with the mundane jobs around the house, with a good deal of light-hearted talk on the part of Sir William and an indulgent chuckle or two from Jolly. She had expected them to leave on Sunday evening, but Sir William had gone into the study and spent a long time on the telephone; when he had come out, it was to announce that his registrar would deal with his cases at the hospital. So she had had another lovely day, with Pauline dressed and up, and Nanny sitting out of her bed for a short while, well enough to want to know what everyone was doing and scattering advice like confetti whenever she had the chance.

She was to telephone Sir William immediately if things should go wrong, or if she felt that everything was getting on top of her. Sir William had kissed Nanny's elderly cheek, hugged his daughter and dropped a casual kiss on Florina's cheek as she stood in the doorway to wave them goodbye. When the car had gone, she put a hand up to her cheek and touched it lightly. She was sure that kissing was quite usual among his kind of people and meant nothing other than a social custom; all the same, it had disturbed her.

The house seemed too large and very empty. Sir William and Jolly had left it in apple-pie order, and on Wednesday Mrs Deakin and Mrs Datchett were to return. So, since Pauline was up for most of the day, there would be very little to do. The week slipped by; Sir William telephoned each evening, talking at length to Pauline, after he had had a brief report from Florina. He would be down on Friday evening, he told her, and he would be coming alone.

With Nanny sitting comfortably beside the Aga and Pauline making a cake for tea, Florina bent her mind to food for the weekend. By the time the car came to a quiet halt before the house, she had a vegetable soup simmering on the Aga, *Boeuf flamand*, rich with beer and onions, in the oven and a strawberry pavlova in the fridge. Moreover, she had put on a clean apron, replaited her hair and done her face with the modest make-up at her disposal.

It was, therefore, disappointing when Sir William, his arm round Pauline's shoulders, wandered into the kitchen, and greeted Nanny warmly before glancing briefly at her with a casual, 'Hello, Florina. I hear that Pauline's made a cake for tea.'

She assented quietly; there was, after all, no need for him to ask how the week had gone; he had phoned each evening and she had given him a faithful account of the day. She made the tea and carried the tray out on to the patio while he went upstairs with Pauline. When they came down again she had shut the kitchen door, put a small tray beside Nanny's chair and gone back to her cooking, a mug of tea on the table beside her. She heard them on the patio presently and went to set the table in the dining-room. The cheerful meals in the kitchen had been all very well, but the circumstances had been unusual. She arranged the glass and silver just so on the starched linen cloth, set a bowl of roses in its centre and stood back to admire the effect.

'Very nice,' said Sir William from the door, 'very elegant. You have a talent for home-making, Florina—your husband will be a lucky man.'

He came into the room and sat on the edge of the table. 'I'm taking Pauline back with me on Sunday—she's going to spend a week with my sister's children at Eastdean, near Brighton. I'll drop her off on my way back to town. Nanny will stay here, but she is well enough to leave alone if you would like to take time off to shop or to go home. You don't mind being on your own with Nanny and Pauline? I've never asked you and I should have done.'

'I know everyone in the village,' she told him, 'and I'm not nervous. Will you be bringing Pauline back next weekend?' She added quickly, in case he thought it was none of her business, 'Just so that I can help her pack enough clothes...'

'We'll be back on Saturday morning; I won't be able to get away from hospital until Friday evening. I'll drive down to my sister's and spend the night. Oh, and I dare say Miss Fortesque will be joining us. She'll drive herself down some time on Saturday, but have lunch ready, will you?'

He wandered over to the door. 'You've had more than your share of hard work since you came here—and no free time, let alone days off. If and when you want a week's holiday, don't hesitate to ask, Florina.' He gave her a kind smile as he went.

In her room that night, getting ready for bed, she pondered a holiday. She couldn't remember when she had last had one—when her mother had been alive and the pair of them had gone to Holland once a year to see her mother's family, and she remembered that with wistful pleasure. After her mother's death, her father had said that there was no point in wasting money on visiting uncles and aunts and cousins whom he hardly knew. She wrote to them regularly in her perfect Dutch, for her mother had been firm about her speaking, writing and reading that language. 'For you are half-Dutch,' she had reminded Florina, 'and I don't want you to forget that.' It was so long now since she had visited her mother's family, but she had liked them and had felt at home in the old-fashioned house just outside Zierikzee. She would like to see them again, but it didn't seem very likely.

Sir William took Pauline for a short drive in the morning, and in the afternoon they sat on the patio, watching the swans below them. Florina, making a batch of congress tarts for tea, could hear them laughing and talking. After tea, before she needed to start cooking for the evening meal, she changed into one of her sensible cotton dresses and went home. Her father greeted her sourly and went back to reading his paper, but her aunt was glad to sit down and have half an hour's gossip. She had settled down nicely, she told Florina, and her father seemed happy enough. 'You've got yourself a nice job, love. That Sir William is spoken of very highly in the village. Had a busy time with the measles, though, didn't you?'

Her father didn't miss her, thought Florina regretfully, as she returned to the Wheel House, but at least she thought he seemed content, and Aunt Meg was happy. She went to the kitchen and started on dinner—avocado pears with a hot cheese sauce, trout caught locally, cooked with almonds, and a summer pudding.

After dinner, Sir William came into the kitchen and told her how much he had enjoyed his meal. He was kind but casual; there was none of the friendliness of the previous week.

He went after lunch the next day, taking Pauline with him; a Pauline who was flatteringly loath to leave Florina behind. The warmth of her goodbyes made up for the casual wave of the hand from her father as they drove off.

It was pleasant to have some leisure. Half-way through the week, Florina left Mrs Datchett to keep Nanny company, and took herself off to Salisbury. She had her wages in her pocket and the summer sales were on. The shops were full of pretty summer dresses, but she went straight to Country Casuals where she found a jacket and skirt in a pleasing shade of peach pink and a matching blouse. She added low-heeled court shoes and a small handbag and left the shop, very well satisfied, even if a good deal lighter in her pocket. There was enough money left over to buy a cotton jersey dress, canvas sandals and some undies, even a new lipstick and a face cream guaranteed to erase wrinkles and bring a bloom to the cheeks of the users. Florina, who hadn't a wrinkle anyway, and owned a skin as clear as a child's, could have saved her money, but it smelled delicious and fulfilled her wish to improve her looks. She wasn't sure why.

She showed everything to Mrs Frobisher when she got back, and then hung her finery in the cupboard in her room, got into one of her sensible, unflattering cotton dresses and went to pick the raspberries. On Friday she would cycle into Wilton and get some melons; halved and filled with the raspberries and heaped with whipped cream and a dash of brandy, they would make a good desert for Sir William and whoever came with him. He hadn't said that he was bringing guests but she must be prepared . . .

He arrived on Saturday morning, with Wanda beside him and a sulky Pauline on the back seat. Mrs Frobisher, on her feet once more, but not doing much as yet, opened the door to them, and Florina heard them talking and laughing in the hall; at least Wanda was laughing. A moment later, the kitchen door was flung open and Pauline danced in.

'Oh, Florina, I have missed you, it's lovely to be here again! Can I make cakes for tea? My aunt has a cook too, but she wouldn't let me go into the kitchen. My cousins are scared of her. I'm not scared of you.'

Florina was piping potato purée into elegant swirls. 'Oh, good! Of course you can make cakes. Any idea what you want to make?'

'Scones—like yours. Daddy says they melt in his mouth . . .'

'OK. Come back about three o'clock, Pauline. I'm going to pick the last of the raspberries after lunch; you can make the scones when I've done that.'

Pauline danced away, and she got on with her cooking, trying not to hear Wanda's voice on the patio, or her trilling laugh. With luck, she wouldn't have to see anything of her over the weekend; Mrs Deakin or Mrs Datchett would be early enough to take her breakfast tray up each morning.

Florina chopped parsley so viciously that Sir William, coming into the kitchen, said in mock alarm, 'Oh, dear, shall I come back later?'

Could she knock up some savoury bits and pieces? he wanted to know. He had asked a few local people in for drinks that evening, and could dinner be put back for half an hour?

On his way out of the kitchen he turned to look at her. 'Quite happy?' he wanted to know.

Her 'Yes, thank you, sir,' was offered without expression. There was no reason for her to be anything else. She had a good job, money in her pocket and a kind, considerate employer. Of course she was happy.

A dozen or so people came for drinks. She knew them by sight; people from the bigger country houses in the vicinity. Doctor Stone and his wife were there too, and the Rector, and the dear old lady from Crow Cottage at the other end of the village whose husband had been the local vet. She lived alone now with several cats and an elderly dog. Florina had made cheese straws, *petits fours* and tiny cheese puffs, while Pauline made the scones. The first batch were a failure; Florina put them into a bowl, observing that the swans would soon dispose of them, and advised Pauline to try again. 'And this time they will be perfect,' she encouraged.

Edible, at any rate! Her father assured her that they were delicious and ate four, and Pauline swelled with pride, although the sight of Wanda taking a bite and then refusing to finish hers took the edge off her pleasure. 'I expect I'm fussy,' said Wanda, laughing gently. Then she shot a look of dislike at Pauline, who wanted to know if she knew how to make scones.

'I have never needed to cook,' she said loftily. 'I have other things with which to occupy my time.'

'It's a good thing that I have the means to employ someone who can, my dear,' observed Sir William, and cut himself a slice of Florina's apple cake. It was as light as a feather and he felt that he deserved it after his small daughter's offering. 'But it is reassuring to know that, should I ever be without a cook, Pauline will at least know an egg from a potato.'

He drove Wanda back to London on Sunday evening, for she refused to get up early on Monday morning so that he might be in the hospital in time for his mid-morning clinic. She was, she declared, quite unable to get up before nine o'clock each morning. Florina heard her saying it and heartily despised her for it. Anyone with any sense knew that one of the best parts of the day was the hour just as the sun was rising. Besides, Sir William was no lie-abed; hospitals, unless she was very much mistaken, started their day early, and that would apply to most of the staff, including the most senior of the consultants.

Pauline came in from the front porch where she had been waving goodbye.

'It's super to be here again just with you and Nanny, only I wish Daddy were here, too.'

'Don't you like your home in London?' asked Florina. She was getting their supper and had made Nanny comfortable in a chair by the Aga.

'Oh, yes, that's super too, only Wanda is always there. She walks in and out as though it were her home, and it isn't, it's Daddy's and mine, and Jolly and Mrs Jolly's of course.' She added, 'Oh, and Shirley, she lives there too. Mrs Peek comes in each day to help, but she goes home after her dinner.'

'It sounds very pleasant,' said Florina a bit absent-mindedly: she was remembering that Wanda hadn't spoken to her at all during the weekend. Sir William hadn't said much, either, but he had thanked her for the bits and pieces she had made for the drinks party, and praised the roast beef she had served up for dinner on Saturday evening. He had also wished her goodbye until the following weekend.

'I'll be alone,' he had told her, 'perhaps we might have a picnic . . . Pauline has rather set her heart on one. You and Nanny, Pauline and I.'

The fine weather held; the three of them picked beans and peas and courgettes and tomatoes, and stocked up the freezer. And, with Pauline on a borrowed bike, Florina cycled with her to Wilton, and they shopped for the weekend and had ices at the little tea room in the High Street.

It was on the Thursday that she had a letter from her Tante Minna in Holland. Florina's cousin Marijke was going to be married, and would she go to the wedding and, if possible, stay for a week or so? It was a long time, wrote Tante Minna in her beautiful copperplate Dutch, since Florina had been to see them, and, while they were aware that her father had no wish to visit them, her family in Holland felt that they should keep in touch. The wedding was to be in a week and a half's time and she hoped to hear...

A wedding, reflected Florina—a chance to wear her new outfit and, since she could afford the fare, there was no reason why she shouldn't accept. Sir William had told her that if she wanted a holiday she had only to ask. He would be back at home on the next day. She spent the rest of the day and a good deal of the night deciding exactly what she would say to him.

He looked tired when he came, but he still remembered to see her in the kitchen and to ask if everything was all right. 'I see Nanny has quite recovered—I hope Pauline hasn't been too much trouble?'

Florina gave a brief résumé of their week, and took in the tea tray.

'Worn to the bone,' commented Nanny as they drank their own tea in the kitchen. 'What he needs is peace and quiet when he gets home of an evening, but that Miss Fortesque is always on at him to go dining and dancing.'

It wasn't the time to ask about holidays, and Florina went to bed feeling frustrated. Perhaps she wouldn't have the chance to ask him, and if she didn't this weekend it would be too late to make arrangements to go to the wedding. She spent a poor night worrying about it, which proved a waste of time for, as she was boiling the kettle for early morning tea, he wandered into the kitchen in trousers and an open-necked shirt.

'Oh, you're up,' she said stupidly, and then, 'Good morning, Sir William.'

'Morning, Florina—too nice to stay in bed—I've been for a walk. Is that tea? Good.' He sat down on the side of the table and watched her, clean and starched and neat, getting mugs and sugar and milk. 'Have a cup with me, I want to talk.'

Her hand shook a little as she poured the milk. The sack? Wanda and he getting married? Something awful she had done?

'I'm wondering if you would like that week's holiday? In a week's time I have to go to Leiden to give a series of lectures, and I thought I would take Pauline with me. Nanny can stay here, and the Jollys can come down and keep her company. Our Shirley is quite happy to look after the house in town, and Mrs Peek will move in while we are away and keep her company...'

He broke off to look at her. Florina was gazing at him, her gentle mouth slightly open, wearing the bemused look of someone who had just received a smart tap on the head. 'In a week's time,' she repeated, a bit breathless. 'Oh, I'll be able to go to the wedding!'

'Yours?' asked Sir William.

She shook her head. 'No—my cousin—they live close to Zierikzee, and she's getting married, and I've been asked to go and it's just perfect! While you are in Leiden, I'll be able to stay with my aunt.'

She beamed at him and then asked soberly, 'That is, if you don't mind?'

He leaned over and poured the tea into two mugs. 'My dear girl, why should I mind? It's the hand of fate, of course you must go. How?'

'Oh, I'll fly, I did it with Mother several times, when she was alive we went each year, Basingstoke, you know, and then a bus to Gatwick...'

Sir William cut himself a slice of bread from the loaf she had put ready for toast. 'I know a better way. When is this wedding?' When she had told him, he said, 'It couldn't be better. We'll give you a lift in the car and drop you off...'

'It's out of your way,' she pointed out.

'A mile or so, besides I've always wanted to take a look at Zierikzee. Can you stay with your aunt until we pick you up on the way home?'

'Yes—oh, yes!' Her face glowed with delight and Sir William took a second look at her. Quite pretty in a quiet, unassuming way, and she had lovely eyes. He got off the table. 'That's settled, then. We'll work out the details later. Can you really be ready for this picnic by eleven o'clock? The New Forest, so Pauline tells me. She has it all planned.'

Florina nodded happily, in a delightful daze, quite unable to stop smiling. Sir William, on the way upstairs to his room, reflected that she was a funny little thing as well as being a marvellous cook. She didn't seem to have much fun, either, and this cousin's wedding would be a treat for her.

CHAPTER FOUR

THE Bentley slid with deceptive speed around the southern outskirts of Salisbury, took the Ringwood road and at Downton turned off to Cadnam. Florina and Nanny, sitting in the back of the car, admired the scenery and listened to Pauline's happy chatter to her father. In Lyndhurst, a few miles further on from Cadnam, they stopped for coffee at an olde-worlde tea-shop, all dark oak and haughty waitresses dressed to match. The coffee was dreadful and Sir William muttered darkly over his, only cheered by Florina's recital of what she and Nanny had packed in the picnic basket.

Just outside the little town they entered the Forest, and presently turned off into a narrow lane which opened out into a rough circle of green grass surrounded by trees. It was pleasantly warm and Pauline pranced off, intent on exploring, taking her father with her. He had hesitated before they went, looking at Florina, but she had no intention of leaving Nanny alone.

'We'll get the lunch ready,' she said firmly, wishing with all her heart that she could go with them.

They were back after half an hour or so, and in the meantime she had spread their picnic on the ground near the car. They had brought a folding chair for Nanny, and she was sitting in it, telling Florina what to do, watching as she set out the little containers with sausage rolls, sandwiches, meat pies and cheese puffs. There was lemonade, too, and beer for Sir William as well as a thermos of hot coffee, and apples and pears. Sir William heaved a sigh of contentment as he made himself comfortable against a tree stump.

'The temptation to retire is very strong,' he observed and, at Florina's surprised look, 'No, I'm not sixty, Florina, although I feel all of that, sometimes.' He bit into a pie. 'This seems as good a time as any to plan out our week in Holland.' He glanced at Mrs Frobisher. 'Nanny, I'm taking Pauline over to Holland with me when I go in a week's time—we'll be gone for a week. The Jollys are coming down to keep you company. You'll like that, won't you? Florina is going to Holland too, to a cousin's wedding, and we'll bring her back with us. Now, how shall we go?' He looked at Florina who, having no idea at all, said nothing. 'Hovercraft, I think, and drive up from Calais.' He finished the pie and started on a sausage roll. 'Have you a passport, Florina? No—well go to the post office in Wilton and get a passport from there. There isn't time for you to get a new one through the normal channels; you'll need the old one for details, though. Pauline's on my passport. Let me see, if we leave Dover about ten o'clock, we should be in Zierikzee during the afternoon, and Amsterdam a couple of hours later. I start lectures on the Monday, so that will fit in very well.'

'Will Pauline be alone?' asked Florina.

'We're staying with friends. She'll have a marvellous time, they have four children.'

It was nice to know that Wanda wasn't to be of the party. Florina poured coffee and allowed her thoughts to dwell on the pleasures in store.

The weekend went too quickly. They all went to church on Sunday morning, and in the evening Sir William drove himself into Wilton to a friend's house for drinks. He had a lot of friends, reflected Florina, concentrating on the making of lemon sauce. In the morning he left early, while Nanny was still in bed. Pauline had come down to say goodbye, but she went back to bed again, leaving Florina to clear away Sir William's breakfast things and start the day's chores. He wouldn't be back until the next weekend, and it seemed a very long time.

Actually, the days passed quickly. Florina needed Pauline's help to gather together suitable clothes to take with her, there were beds to be made up and the house to be left in apple-pie order for the Jollys' arrival. There was her own wardrobe to decide upon; she would be able to wear her new clothes, but they would need to be augmented. Sir William phoned most evenings to talk to Pauline but, although he spoke to Nanny once or twice, he evinced no desire to speak to Florina.

He arrived rather late on Friday evening, and Jolly and his wife drove down at the same time in the other car. Pauline, already in bed, came bouncing down to fling her arms around his neck. 'We're all ready,' she assured him excitedly, 'and Florina is ready too, and she's filled the fridge with food that means Mrs Jolly won't have to bother too much. She washed her hair this afternoon and she did mine last night.'

She skipped away to greet the Jollys. 'There is supper for you and we put flowers in your bedroom.'

'Bed for you, Pauline,' said Nanny severely, appearing to greet Sir William and the Jollys. 'The child is excited,' she told Sir William.

'So am I, Nanny,' He went past her, into the kitchen where Florina was putting the finishing touches to the salad.

'Busy as usual?' he observed kindly. 'All ready for your holiday, Florina? I do wonder what on earth you'll do with yourself without your cooking stove?'

She smiled politely; she wasn't a girl to him, just the cook—it was a mortifying thought. She thrust it from her, and said soberly, 'Well, I haven't seen my family for some time, Sir William. I expect there will be a lot to talk about.'

That sounded dull enough, she thought crossly. If only he could see her, dressed in her new clothes, being chatted up by some handsome Dutch cousin—only all her cousins were either married or with no looks to speak of; and when would he see her anyway?

She wished that he would go away, not stand there looking at her in that faintly surprised fashion. It disturbed her, although she didn't know why.

They left very early on Sunday morning, driving through the still-sleeping village, past the pub, her home, the farm opposite the bridge and along the narrow country lane which would lead them to Wilton.

She had spent an afternoon with her father during the week, but he hadn't been particularly interested in her plans. She could do as she wished, he had observed grumpily, and he hadn't even expressed the hope that she would enjoy herself. Everyone else had; even Nanny, so sparing in her praise, had told her that she had earned a holiday. 'And I just hope you meet a nice young man,' she had added.

Florina, sitting in the back of the car, bubbling over with excitement, hoped that she would too. If she met a nice young man, then perhaps Sir William wouldn't seem quite so important in her life.

They had an uneventful, very comfortable journey. It made a great difference, she reflected, if you had money. You stopped when you wanted to at good hotels for coffee and lunch, with no need to look at the price list outside to see if you could afford it. Moreover you spoke French in France and when you reached Holland you switched to Dutch, which, while basic, got you what you wanted without any fuss. And you did all that with the calm assurance which was Sir William.

They were crossing the Zeeland Brug by mid-afternoon, glimpsing Zierikzee ahead of them. On dry land once more, Sir William said, over his shoulder, 'You must tell me where to go, Florina. It's outside the town, isn't it?'

She leaned forward, the better to speak to him. 'Yes, go straight on, don't turn into Zierikzee, go to the roundabout and take the road to Drieschor; Schudderbeurs is about two miles...'

The road was straight and narrow, snaking away into the distance. The sign to the village was small and anyone going too fast would miss it. Sir William slowed down when she warned him, and turned left down a narrow lane, joining a pleasant, leafy lane with a handful of cottages and villas on either side of it. There was an old-fashioned country house standing well back from the road with a wide sweep before it. As they went past it Sir William said, 'That looks pleasant; it's an hotel, too...'

'Yes. It's quite well known. I've never been there, it's expensive, but I believe it's quite super... My aunt lives just along that lane to the right.'

There were a handful of houses ringing the edge of wooded country, not large, but well maintained and with fair-sized gardens.

'It's this one.'

Sir William stopped, got out and opened her door. A door in the house opened at the same time and

Tante Minna, looking not a day older than when Florina had seen her five years or more ago, came down the garden path. She had begun to talk the moment she had seen them; she was still talking when she opened the gate and hugged Florina, at the same time casting an eye over Sir William and Pauline. Florina disentangled herself gently. 'Tante Minna, how lovely to see you . . .' She had slipped into Dutch without a conscious effort. 'This is Sir William, I'm his cook, as I told you, and this is his daughter Pauline. They are on their way to Leiden and kindly gave me a lift.'

She had already told Aunt Minna all that in her letter, but she was wishful to bridge an awkward gap.

Tante Minna transferred her twinkling gaze to Sir William. Her English was adequate, about as adequate as his Dutch. They shook hands warmly and Tante Minna turned her attention to Pauline, and then took her by the arm and turned towards the house. 'You will take tea? It is ready. You will like to see my cat and her five kittens?'

They went into the house, light and airy and comfortably furnished. She said in Dutch to Florina, 'Will you explain that your Uncle Constantine is in Goes? Marijke and Jan and Pieter are here, though, and Felix Troost—his father is a partner in your uncle's firm. I believe you met him years ago . . .'

Florina translated, leaving out the bit about Felix Troost, and they went into the sitting-room where Florina was instantly enveloped in a round of handshaking and kissing, emerging to find Sir William talking easily to Felix, whose English was a good deal better than Sir William's Dutch. Pauline had disappeared with Florina's aunt, doubtless in search of the kittens. Indeed, she reappeared a few minutes later with a small fluffy creature tucked under one arm.

Her cousins hadn't changed much, Florina decided; Marijke, a year or two younger than herself, was plump and fair and pretty, good-natured and easy-going, Jan and Pieter, who had still been at school when she had last seen them, were young men now, towering over her, calling her little Rina and wanting to know why she wasn't married. But when the tea tray was brought in, the talk became general, while they drank the milkless tea in small porcelain cups and nibbled thin, crisp biscuits. Not very substantial for Sir William's vast frame, thought Florina, watching him, completely at his ease, discussing their journey with Pieter. He looked up, caught her eye and smiled, and she felt a pleasant glow spreading under her ribs.

He and Pauline left soon, for they still had rather more than an hour's drive ahead of them across the islands to Rotterdam, and then a further hour on the motorway to Amsterdam. But before they went Sir William sat himself down by Florina. 'We'll fetch you next Saturday,' he reminded her. 'I'd like to get to Wheel House in the fairly early evening, so we should leave here not later than two o'clock. Will you be ready then?'

'Yes, of course, Sir William. Would you like coffee here before we go?'

He shook his head. 'No time. We can have a quick stop on the way if we must. He stood up. 'Have a good holiday, Florina. I envy you the peace and quiet here.'

She had forgotten that he was to give lectures for most of the week, and Amsterdam, delightful though it was, was also noisy. She said quietly, 'Perhaps you will be able to spare the time to spend a few days in the country—somewhere like Schudderbeurs, the *hostellerie* is quite famous, you know.'

'Yes, perhaps one day I'll do that.' He patted her shoulder and went out to his car with Pieter and Jan, leaving Pauline to say goodbye.

'I hope I shall like it,' she said uncertainly. 'Daddy won't be there for most of the day...'

'You'll have a gorgeous time,' said Florina cheerfully. 'We'll compare notes when we meet next Saturday, and think how nice it is for your father to have you for company.'

Pauline brightened. 'Yes, he likes me to be with him, that's why I don't see why he needs to marry Wanda. She hates quiet places, she likes to dance and go to the shops and theatre and have people to dinner.'

'Ah, well, perhaps she will change when your father marries her!' Florina kissed the pretty little face, and then walked out to the car and stood with her aunt and cousins, waving until it was out of sight.

'A very nice man,' commented Tante Minna. 'He is married?'

'No, but he is going to be—to a very lovely girl called Wanda.'

'And you do not like her, I think?' asked her aunt, sharp as a needle.

'Well, I don't think she's right for him. He works very hard and I believe he likes his work; it's a part of his life, if you know what I mean. She enjoys the bright lights and I think she's annoyed because he's just come to live at Wheel House—and you know how quiet the village is, Tante Minna! He has a house in London, too, though I don't know where it is, but he likes to spend his weekends at Wheel House, if he can.' She paused, 'And Pauline doesn't like her.'

'It seems that he needs to be rescued,' observed Tante Minna, and added briskly, 'Come indoors, child, and tell us all your news—it's so long...'

Florina made short work of that for, of course, what they really wanted to talk about was the wedding. Marijke took her upstairs to show her her wedding dress, and when they joined the family again she was regaled with the details of the ceremony, Christiaan's job, the flat they would live in and the furniture they had bought for it. Which reminded Florina to go upstairs to the small bedroom at the back of the house and fetch the present she had brought with her. Place mats, rather nice ones, depicting the English countryside, and received with delight by her cousin. Christiaan came then, and they had their evening meal with Oom Constantine, and when it was finished Felix Troost arrived again. He had been in Goes with Florina's uncle, he explained, but had had to call on someone on the way home. He was a good-looking young man, with blue eyes, set rather too close together, and a good deal of very fair hair. He was obviously at home there, and he greeted Florina with a slightly overdone charm. They shook hands and exchanged polite greetings, and she decided then and there that she didn't like him.

A feeling that she became uncertain of as the evening progressed, for he was casually friendly, talking about his work, wanting to know about her life in England. She must have been mistaken in the sudden feeling of dislike that she had had when they met, she reflected as she got ready for bed. Anyway, she would be seeing a good deal of him while she was staying with Tante Minna, and he would be at the wedding and the reception afterwards at the hotel. She allowed her thoughts to dwell on the peach-pink outfit with some satisfaction. It was a pity that Sir William wouldn't see her in her finery. She wondered what he was doing; dining and dancing probably, with some elegant creature whose dress would make the peach-pink look like something run up by the local little dressmaker. She sighed sadly, not knowing why she was sad.

Everyone was up early the next morning and, although the wedding wasn't until mid-afternoon, there was a constant coming and going of family and friends. Florina, nicely made up and wearing the peach-pink, greeted aunts and uncles and cousins she hadn't seen for years, exclaiming over engagements, new babies and the various ailments of the more elderly. She blossomed out under observations that she had grown into quite a presentable young woman, for, as one elderly aunt observed in a ringing voice everyone could hear, 'A plain child you were, Florina. Your mother despaired of you. Never thought you'd get yourself a husband . . . engaged, are you?'

Black beady eyes studied her, and she blushed a little and was eternally grateful to Felix, who flung an arm round her shoulders and said, 'She's waiting for a good honest Dutchman to ask her, aren't you, Florina?' And he kissed her on one cheek. Everyone laughed then, and she decided that she had been mistaken about Felix; he had sounded warmly friendly and he had been kind . . .

With the prospect of the wedding reception later on in the day, no one ate much of the lunch Aunt Minna provided. Guests were to go straight to the *Gemeentehuis*, but even the most distant relations who weren't seen from one year to the next came to the house, so that there was a good deal of good-natured confusion. Deciding who was to go in whose car took considerable time, and presently Florina found herself sitting beside Felix in his BMW with two elderly aunts on the back seat. It was the last to leave in the procession of cars, leaving Marijke, following the time-honoured custom, to wait for her bridegroom to fetch her from her home, bearing the bridal bouquet.

The *Gemeentehuis* was the centre of interest, and the congestion in the narrow street was making it worse than ever to drive through the little town. The guests trooped up the narrow steps into the ancient building and made their way to the Bride Chamber, a handsome apartment at the top of a broad staircase. Florina was urged into a seat in the front row of chairs, since she was a cousin of the bride, while Felix, being a family friend, found his way to a seat at the back, but not before giving her hand a squeeze and whispering that he would drive her to the church presently. She nodded, not really listening, for Marijke and Christiaan were taking their places in front of the *Burgermeester* and the short ceremony started.

Florina, watching closely, thought it seemed too businesslike. It certainly wouldn't do for her. She was glad that Marijke had wanted a church wedding as well, not that she herself was likely to marry, whether in Holland or in England. She didn't know any men, only Felix, and she didn't know him at all really, and Sir William, who didn't count, for he was going to marry Wanda. She fell to day-dreaming of some vague, faceless man who would meet her and fall in love with her at once and they would marry. These musings led, naturally enough, to what she would wear: cream satin, yards of it and a tulle veil. Marijke was wearing a picture hat trimmed with roses, and her dress was white lace. Florina had helped her to dress and had zipped the dress up, only after having urged her cousin to breathe in while she did so, for Marijke was a shade too plump for it. All the same, she looked delightful and her pinched waist had given her a most becoming colour. They were signing the register now, and a few minutes later the whole party followed the bride and groom out to the long line of cars.

The church was barely two minutes' drive, behind the Apple Market, bordering on the big market square, so that the entire wedding party could park in comfort before filing inside. It was a *Hervormdekerk*, and the service was sober and the short homily delivered sternly by the *Dominee*. Florina allowed her attention to wander, stealthily checking on the congregation, refreshing her memory as to who they were. She had forgotten over the years what a very large family her mother had; sitting there in the church she felt more Dutch than English. Her eye, roaming round the church, lighted upon Felix who smiled and nodded. He seemed like an old friend, and she smiled back, stifling the vague feeling of dislike she had for him.

The service ended and the bride and groom got into their flower-decked car and started on their slow tour of the town before driving back to Schudderbeurs, while everyone else went back to the *hostellerie*.

The wedding party was to be held in the large room built at the back of the hotel. It had been decorated with pot plants and flowers, and a buffet had been nicely arranged on a long table at one end. The afternoon was still warm and sunny, and the doors on to the garden had been opened so that the guests could spill outside. Florina, driven back by Felix, stood taking breaths of fresh air, listening idly to his rather conceited talk about himself and his work. He was doing his best to impress her, but she didn't feel impressed; indeed, she was shocked to find that she was bored. Suddenly she wanted to be back at Wheel House, busy at the stove while Sir William sat on the kitchen table, polishing off the scones she had made for tea.

She heard Felix say in a cocksure manner, 'And, of course, I shall be a partner in a year or so.' He gave a self-deprecating laugh. 'You can't keep a good man down, you know!'

She murmured politely and was glad that the bridal pair had arrived and everyone could sit down and eat the delicious food the hotel had provided. There was champagne, of course, and speeches. No wedding cake, for that wasn't the custom in Holland, but little dishes of chocolates and sweetmeats and more champagne. Presently, friends and acquaintances arrived, each with a present or flowers, to wish the bride and groom every happiness, and join in the dancing. It was great fun, reflected Florina, her ordinary face glowing with warmth and excitement, whirling around the floor with cousins and uncles and Felix; Felix more than anyone else, but what with the champagne and the cheerful, noisy party, she was content to dance the night away. She hadn't enjoyed herself so much for years.

Presently, the newly wedded pair disappeared in the direction of the little white house in the hotel grounds, where they would spend the night before driving to their new flat in Goes on the following day. It was only in recent years that newly marrieds had abandoned the custom of going straight to their new home from the wedding reception. The little white house was much in demand among the young people, some of them coming from miles around.

The dancing went on for another hour or more before the guests finally left. Some of the more elderly were staying at the *hostellerie* for the night, the younger ones were either putting up with friends in the village or driving home through the night. Florina walked the short distance to her aunt's house, arm in arm with a bevy of cousins and Felix. He was to spend what remained of the night with friends in the village, and he parted from them on the doorstep, but not before he had asked her to spend the next day with him.

When she had hesitated, he had promised, 'We won't do anything strenuous, and I won't come round until eleven o'clock.'

And when she still hesitated, her cousins joined in. 'Oh, go on, Rina, none of us will want to do anything tomorrow, and you'll enjoy a day out.'

She wasn't too happy about it as she tumbled into bed, perhaps because she was tired. Besides, she could always change her mind in the morning.

She didn't; she was awake only a little later than usual and it was a glorious morning. There were only four days left of her holiday—she must make the most of them. She had a shower and dressed in the cotton jersey and went down to the roomy kitchen. Her aunt was already up; there was coffee on the stove and a basket of rolls and croissants on the table.

'Going out with Felix?' asked Tante Minna.

Florina nodded. 'You don't mind? He's not coming until eleven o'clock—I'll give you a hand around the house—you must be tired . . .'

'Yes, but it was a splendid wedding, wasn't it, *liefje*? When shall we see you marry, I wonder?'

Florina bit into a roll; Tante Minna was awfully like her mother. She felt her throat tighten at the thought but she answered lightly, 'I've no idea, but I promise that you shall dance at my wedding if every I have one...'

'Do they dance at English weddings?'

'Oh, rather, discotheques, the same as here.' But she wouldn't want that—only a quiet wedding in the church at home, and a handful of family and friends and, of course, the bridegroom—that vague but nebulous figure she could never put a face to. She finished her roll and tidied away her breakfast things and then, armed with a duster, set about bringing the sitting-room to that peak of pristine perfection which Tante Minna, wedding or no wedding, expected.

Presently her uncle appeared to drink his coffee and then go into the garden to inspect his roses, and after him, Felix, flamboyantly dressed, oozing charm and impatient of the coffee Tante Minna insisted on them having before they went. Florina got into the car beside him, told her aunt that they would be back in good time for the evening meal, eaten as was customary at six o'clock, and sat quietly while Felix roared through the tiny village and on to the road to Browershaven, away from Zierikzee.

The day wasn't a success. Felix talked about himself and, what was more, in a lofty fashion which Florina found tedious. He had no clear idea where they were going, but drove around the surrounding countryside in a haphazard fashion, and when she had suggested mildly that it would be nice to go to the coast he said, 'Oh, you don't want to walk on the beach, for heaven's sake.'

'Then what about Veere or Domburg?'

'Packed out. We'll go inland and find a place to eat, and park the car somewhere quiet and get to know each other.'

Florina wished that she hadn't come, but it was too late to do anything about it now. They stopped at a small roadside café, full of local men playing billiards and, unlike most Dutch cafés, not over-clean. She lingered over her *limonade* and kaas broodje, uneasy at the amount of beer Felix was drinking. With good reason, she was to discover, for, once more in the car, he stopped after a few miles and flung an arm around her shoulders.

Florina removed the arm and eyed him severely. 'Tante Minna expects me back before six o'clock, so be good enough to start back now. I'm sorry if I disappoint you, but I came with you for a pleasant day out and that's all.'

She was aware that she sounded priggish, even in Dutch, but she wasn't prepared for his snarling, 'Prudish little bitch—no wonder you haven't got a man. I wish you joy of your cooking. That's all you're fit for.'

Neither of them spoke again until they reached Tante Minna's house, and when Florina said goodbye in a cold voice Felix didn't answer.

'Had a nice day?' asked her aunt. Seeing her stony face, she added hastily, 'We are all going to Goes the day after tomorrow. You'll come won't you, *liefje*? Just the family—Marijke wants us all to see their flat.'

The last day of her holiday was pure pleasure. On Thursday, she joined a happy gathering of family at a proud Marijke's new home, which was smothered in flowers and pot plants from friends and such members of the family who hadn't been able to attend the wedding. Florina admired everything, drank a little too much wine, ate the *bitterballen* served with it, and agreed that the bridal bouquet, hung on the wall at the head of the bed, was the most beautiful she had ever seen. Presently, she sat down with everyone else to *nasi goreng* and an elaborate dessert of ice-cream. A day to remember, she assured her uncle when he wanted to know if she had enjoyed her holiday.

Sir William had said that he would pick her up after lunch on Saturday. She was up early to pack her small case, eat her roll and sliced cheese and drink her aunt's delicious coffee, before wheeling out her aunt's elderly bike from the garage and setting off for a last ride with Jan and Pieter. They went to Zierikzee to start with and had more coffee. Then they went on to Haamstede and cycled on to the lighthouse, where they sat in the sun and ate ice-creams. The morning had gone too quickly, as last mornings always do; they had to ride fast in order to get back to Tante Minna's in time for the midday lunch.

It was a leisurely meal, for there was time enough before Sir William would arrive. Presently, Florina did the last of her packing and closed her case. She did her face and hair too, anxious not to keep him waiting. She went to wait downstairs and found, to her annoyance, that Felix was there.

There was nothing in his manner to remind her of their last meeting; he greeted her as though they had parted the best of friends, and began as soon as he could to talk of the possibility of meeting her again. 'Mustn't lose sight of you,' he observed smugly, and flung an unwanted arm across her shoulders.

Florina edged away, and went into the garden on the pretext of saying goodbye to her uncle, but he followed her outside, seemingly intent on demonstrating that they were the best of friends, and more than that. He was standing with her when the Bentley slowed to a silent halt on the other side of the hedge. Florina, talking to her uncle, didn't see it at once, but

Felix did; he put an arm round her waist and drew her close, and Sir William, getting out of his car, couldn't help but see it.

He turned away at once to say something to Pauline, so missing Florina's indignant shove as she pushed Felix away. At the same time, she saw the car, and a moment later Sir William, strolling towards her aunt's front door. The wealth of feeling which surged through her at the sight of him took her by surprise. He had been at the back of her thoughts all the while she had been at Tante Minna's but she hadn't understood why, but now she knew. *He* was the vague man of her day-dreams, the man she loved, had fallen in love with, not knowing it, weeks ago; ever since she had first set eyes on him, she realised with astonishment.

She hurried to meet him, thoughts tumbling about her head. It was bliss to see him again, but never, never must she show her feelings, although just at that moment she longed above all things to rush at him and fling her arms around his neck. This last thought was so horrifying that she went a bright pink, and looked so guilty that Sir William frowned at his own thoughts.

He glanced at Felix, decided that he didn't much like the look of him and countered Florina's breathless, 'Sir William...' with a pleasantly cool, 'Ah, Florina, we have arrived at the wrong moment. My apologies...'

This remark stopped her in her tracks. 'Wrong moment? I'm quite ready to leave, Sir William...'

'But not, perhaps, willing?'

She gaped at him, and when Felix sidled up to her and put an arm round her shoulders she barely noticed it. At that moment, Pauline came prancing over to fling her arms around her neck and declare that she was over the moon to see her darling Florina again.

There was a polite flurry of talk, then coffee was offered and refused, and goodbyes said. Presently, Florina found herself in the back of the car, listening to Pauline's chatter. Sir William was, for the most part, silent, but when he did make some casual remark it was in his usual placid manner. He asked no questions of Florina about her holiday and she, suddenly shy of him, sat tongue-tied. What should have been a happy end to her holiday was proving to be just the opposite. Her newly discovered love was bubbling away inside her. Although she knew that he had no interest in her, he had always treated her with what she had thought was friendship and she was willing to settle for that, but now she had the feeling that behind his placid manner there was a barrier.

To brood over her fancies was of no use, so she bestirred herself to listen to Pauline's plans: picnics and mushrooming and cycling with Florina and cookery lessons . . .

'Wanda will be staying with us for at least a week,' said her father. 'You'll be able to go out with her if I am not at home.'

Pauline made a face over her shoulder to Florina, who smiled in a neutral fashion. The smile froze when Sir William added pleasantly, 'Florina has a job to do, Pauline. You mustn't monopolise her free time.'

That remark, thought Florina, puts me nicely in my place.

CHAPTER FIVE

THEY arrived back at Wheel House to a most satisfyingly warm welcome. The journey had gone smoothly, although Florina, knowing Sir William, would have been surprised if it had been otherwise. She had spent the greater part of the journey alternately day-dreaming and worrying as to why his manner towards her had become so cool—still friendly, but she had to admit it was the friendliness of an employer towards an employee.

They all sat down to supper round the kitchen table, talking cheerfully with Sir William asking questions of Jolly and being given a résumé of the week's happenings. Presently, an excited Pauline was escorted off to bed by Nanny, and Sir William turned to Jolly.

'I'll need to be away by seven o'clock at the latest. I'd like you and Mrs Jolly to drive back at the same time. I've a list for ten o'clock, so I'll offload my bag at the house and go straight on to the hospital. I'll not be back for lunch, and I'm taking Miss Fortesque out to dinner—if there is anything you want me for, I'll be home round about tea time.'

Florina said, in a colourless voice, 'Would you like breakfast at half-past six, Sir William?'

'We shan't need you, Florina. Mrs Jolly will see to that.' He added, in a kind, impersonal voice, '*You* must be tired, why don't you go to bed?'

So she went, exchanging polite goodnights. There had been no chance to thank him for taking her to Holland, and he had evinced no wish to know if she had enjoyed herself, but then, why should he? She was the cook and she had better remember that. Besides, she had no part in his life; Wanda had that. She cried herself to sleep and woke early to listen to the Jollys quietly leaving the room on the other side of the landing. Presently she smelled the bacon frying and the fragrance of toast, and heard the murmur of voices. Her window gave her a view of the road running through the village, providing she craned her neck, and soon she saw the two cars disappearing on their way to London.

Sir William had given her no instructions, but when she went downstairs later and started to clear the table and lay it again for their breakfast, Nanny joined her.

'You didn't have much to say for yourself at supper,' she observed, her sharp eyes studying Florina's swollen eyelids. 'Wasn't your holiday all you'd hoped for?' She added, 'Did you want to stay in Holland?'

'No. Oh, no! And I had a super time. It was a lovely wedding, and it was so nice to see everyone again. It is lovely to be back, though . . .'

Nanny grunted. 'Well, I missed you, for what it's worth.' She accepted the cup of tea that Florina offered, and sat down by the open door. 'Sir William won't be back until Friday evening, and Miss Fortesque's coming with him. He intends to give a small dinner party on Saturday—six, I think he said, and if the weather is fine he wants to take a picnic up on to Bulbarrow Down. He's asked the Meggisons from Butt House—they've three children, haven't they? Company for Pauline. He said he would telephone during the week about the food.' She passed her cup and Florina refilled it. 'He said to have a quiet week and to see that Pauline got out of doors. If she wants to go to Salisbury she may, he says, provided that one of us goes with her. She will be starting school soon.' Nanny looked round the pleasant kitchen. 'I shall miss this...'

Florina, slicing bread for toast, looked up, startled. 'Mrs Frobisher—you're not going away?'

'Just as soon as that Miss Fortesque can persuade Sir William that I'm not needed.' There was a pause and the stern, elderly voice wavered slightly. 'With Pauline at school, she'll say that there's nothing for me to do...'

'But that's rubbish!' cried Florina. 'You see to the silver and the mending, and keep the accounts and look after everything.'

'I do my best, but it's my opinion that once they're married she'll pack Pauline off to a boarding-school and come down here as little as possible.'

'But Sir William loves this house. I dare say he has a beautiful home in London, too, but you can love two houses... Besides, he works so hard, and he can do what he likes here.'

If Nanny found Florina's outburst surprising, she gave no sign. She said, 'Well he's old enough and wise enough to know what he wants, but he deserves better. His first marriage wasn't happy—he married too young. I told him so at the time, and I'll make no bones about saying that it was a relief when she was killed in a car accident, gallivanting off with one of her men friends while he worked. A bad wife, and a worse mother, poor young woman.' She gave Florina a quick look. 'I can't think why I'm telling you all this, but you're fond of Pauline, aren't you, and you like Sir William?'

'Oh, yes,' said Florina, putting so much feeling into the two words that Nanny nodded gently, well aware why she had unburdened herself. One never knew, she thought, and there was no harm in spying out the land, as it were. Florina had come back from Holland sad and too quiet, and Sir William had been holding down some problem or other behind that placid face of his—no one was going to tell her different. She had known him all his life, hadn't she? And she wouldn't let anyone tell her not to interfere if she saw the chance.

'Well, have you any plans for today?' she asked briskly.

'Well, I'll go through the cupboards, then go up to the farm shop if we are short of anything. Perhaps Pauline...'

She was interrupted by the little girl dancing into the kitchen to hug first Nanny and then her.

'It's marvellous to be back!' she declared. 'I want to go cycling—Florina, do say you will, and we can go into Wilton and buy Daddy a birthday present.'

She inspected the table. 'Oh, good, it's scrambled eggs—I'm famished. Daddy woke me to say goodbye. Did he say goodbye to you, Florina?'

'No, dear, but I'm sure he won't mind us going into Wilton. When do you want to go?'

The week passed too quickly. There was so much to do: the swans to feed, the Meggison children to visit for tea, long rambling walks to take and the promised visit to Wilton. Sir William telephoned each evening, but it wasn't until Thursday that he asked to speak to Florina.

He began without preamble. 'Florina, Miss Fortesque and I will be down on Friday evening, so lay on a good dinner, will you? There will be six of us for dinner on Saturday. Any ideas?'

She had been listening to his calm voice, but not his words. With a great effort, she tore her thoughts away from him and mentally thumbed through her cookery books. 'Watercress soup? Grilled trout with pepper sauce? Fillets of lamb with rosemary and thyme and *pommes lyonnaises* and a fresh tomato purée . . .' She thought for a moment. 'I've got pears in wine or peaches in brandy . . .'

'My dear girl—my mouth is watering. It sounds splendid. About the picnic on Sunday—shall I leave that to you?'

She said sedately, 'Very well, Sir William. Just lunch?'

'Yes—we'll be back for one of your splendid teas.' He rang off, leaving her quiet, and quite certain that she was going to be so busy at the weekend that she would barely glimpse him, let alone speak to him. Although what did that matter? she reflected sadly. She was the cook and let her never forget it.

With female perversity, she dragged her hair back into a severe plait on Saturday, didn't bother with make-up and, once the serious business of preparing dinner was finished, went to her room and got into a freshly starched dress and white apron. Pauline, prancing into the kitchen to see what there was for tea, stopped short at the sight of her.

'Florina, how severe you look! And you've forgotten your lipstick.'

'No time,' said Florina briskly, taking a fruitcake from the Aga. 'There are some fairy cakes on the table, and I've made strawberry jam sandwiches. Don't eat too much or you won't want your dinner.'

Pauline gave her a look of affection. 'You sound just like a mum,' she observed. 'Do you suppose Wanda will be a nice mum?'

'Oh, I expect so,' lied Florina briskly. She would be awful, she thought, no sticky fingers, no quick cuddles with grubby toddlers. There would be a nursemaid, young and not in the least cosy, and the children would be on show for half an hour after tea. She wondered if Sir William would stand for that; that's if there *were* any more children.

'You look so sad,' said Pauline, 'ever since you left Holland.'

Nanny had said the same thing, reflected Florina. She would have to mend her ways or leave. Unthinkable! 'Well, I'm not.' She made her voice sound cheerful. 'Sit down for a minute and tell me what you would like to have to eat on this picnic.'

Sir William arrived soon after six o'clock, with Wanda exquisite in an outfit in cyclamen and hunter's green; not in the least suitable for a weekend in a small country village, but guaranteed to give its inhabitants something to talk about for a few days.

She got out of the car and went into the house ahead of him, calling in a petulant voice, 'Where's everyone? I want my bags taken up to my room; I'm not fit to be seen!'

She paused by the passage leading to the kitchen and addressed Florina's back, busy at the Aga.

'Cook, leave that, and get my things from the car.'

Florina took no notice; she was at the precise point when the sauce she was making would either be a triumph of culinary art or an inedible failure.

She didn't turn round when she heard Sir William say, 'Florina has her work, Wanda. You can't expect her to leave it to carry your cases. I'll bring them up in a moment.'

Florina heard his laughing greeting to Pauline, their voices fading as they went out to the car. He had always come to the kitchen to ask her how she was, but this evening he didn't, perhaps because he had gone upstairs with Wanda's cases. She knew soon enough that that wasn't so, for she heard him talking to Nanny in the hall. She went about the business of dinner: mushrooms cooked in wine and cream for starters, minute steaks with duchesse potatoes and braised celery, lemon sorbet and Bavarian creams with lashings of cream. She had baked rolls, too, and curled the farm butter and arranged a cheeseboard. To please Wanda, she had made a dish of carrot straws, shreds of celery, slivers of cabbage and apple. She had made home-made chocolates, too, to go with the coffee, something she knew Pauline would like.

There was half an hour before she needed to dish up, so she slipped up to her room and tidied her hair. Then, since there was no one about, she went out to the patio. It was a lovely evening, turning to dusk, and the white swans were gliding away to settle for the night. A bat or two skimmed past, and somewhere in the distance an owl hooted. From the nearby pub there were muted sounds of cheerful talk and laughter. A peaceful rural scene; no wonder Sir William liked to spend his weekends in his lovely country home. Florina fell to wondering about his house in London; in its way it was probably as charming as Wheel House. Well, she would never see it, nor would she know more of his life than she did now, and that was precious little.

She gave a great sigh and then spun round as Sir William said from the drawing-room door. 'Hello, Florina, you look sad. Did you leave your heart in Holland?'

She stammered a little. 'Oh, good evening, Sir William. No no, of course not...' She retreated to the kitchen door. 'I was just waiting here before I dish up—I hope you don't mind?'

He said testily. 'Mind? Why should I mind? You have as much right to be here as I. Has Pauline been plaguing you?'

'Heavens, no, she's a dear child! We've had such fun, biking and walking and she likes to cook.' She hesitated. 'I suppose she couldn't have a dog or a cat? She loves animals—the swans come when she calls, and we were at the farm the other day when the Jersey cow calved—you don't mind?'

'I entirely approve, Florina, and of course we'll have a dog—*and* a cat. She will have to look after them while I'm in London. Of course when she's at school, you will have to do the looking after.'

'I'll enjoy that—she'll be so happy.'

He said thoughtfully, 'I should have thought of it for myself.'

'I think that you have a great deal to think of, Sir William?' She forgot everything for a moment and gave him a sweet, loving look, and he stared back at her without speaking.

'It's time to dish up.' She was suddenly shy, anxious to get back to the kitchen. But presently, through the open door, she heard Pauline come on to the patio and her squeals of delight when she was told about the dog and cat.

Her delight wasn't echoed by Wanda, who had wandered into the drawing-room unsuitably dressed in flame-coloured taffeta. 'I loathe cats, and I detest dogs with their filthy paws. There'll be neither, Pauline, so you can forget it.'

Florina, in the dining-room, setting the soup tureen on the serving-table, stopped to listen.

'I'm afraid you'll have to overcome your dislike, Wanda.' Sir William sounded at his most placid. 'I have promised Pauline that she shall have them.'

'Well, don't expect me to come here...'

His quiet, 'Very well, my dear,' made her pause.

'Oh, darling, don't be unkind—after all, I bury myself down here in this God-forsaken hole just to please you.'

He sounded interested. 'Is that how it seems to you?'

Wanda pouted prettily. 'No decent restaurants within miles, nowhere to go dancing, no shops. You've no idea what sacrifices I'm making for you, my angel.'

'You would like us to live in town permanently?'

Wanda gave a little crow of delight. 'There! I knew you would see it my way.'

'You're mistaken, Wanda. We'll have to talk about it later on.' He put an arm round his daughter's shoulders. 'Next weekend, we'll have a look for a cat and a dog.'

Florina glanced at the clock, and skipped to the hall to tap on the door and sound the dinner gong. It wasn't quite time, but she considered that intervention of some sort would be a good idea. That wasn't the last of it, however. Long after dinner was finished and Pauline was in bed, as Florina and Nanny were clearing away their own meal, Wanda came into the kitchen.

'I suppose it was you who put Pauline up to badgering her father for cats and dogs? Well, Cook, you can take it from me, once Sir William and I are married I'll get rid of them, and you'll go at the same time.'

Nanny drew in a hissing breath, ready to do battle, but Florina forestalled her. 'I should think Sir William will wish to be consulted before you do anything so unwise, Miss Fortesque. And in any case, I've no intention of listening to your threats.'

Wanda glared back at her, her eyes, narrow slits of dislike. 'Wormed your way in, haven't you?' she observed spitefully. 'Just because you can cook—you're only a servant...'

She stopped when she heard Sir William's footsteps crossing the hall.

'I was just telling Cook how delicious dinner was.'

She turned her back on the kitchen and hooked an arm through his. 'How about a stroll before bed, darling?'

'The hussy!' Nanny's rather dry voice was full of indignation. 'If he only knew what was going on...'

'Well, there is nothing we can do about it, Mrs Frobisher.' Florina began to set the table for breakfast and found that she was shaking with rage.

'Huh!' Nanny put a great deal of feeling into the sound. 'But Sir William is no fool and he has got eyes in his head—I'm not despairing.'

But Florina was; she might love him with her whole heart, but she was powerless to do anything about it. Especially now that he had somehow contrived to put a barrier between them. And what could she have done? If she had been as attractive as Wanda and as beautifully dressed and, moreover, living in Sir William's world, she would have made no bones about competing with Wanda. But famous paediatricians didn't fall in love with their cooks, not in real life, anyway. She laid the last plate tidily in its place and offered to make Nanny a cup of tea before she went to bed.

Pauline spent a good deal of the following morning in the kitchen. She had refused to go to Salisbury with her father and Wanda, who declared that she had to do some urgent shopping. Florina suggested that she should make cakes for tea, and went on with her own preparations for dinner. Lunch was to be cold and there was a raised pie she had made on the previous day, and a salad. She would have an hour to spare in the afternoon, and she planned to go and see her father.

With the exception of Wanda, they had shared breakfast round the kitchen table, and Sir William had gone off with Pauline directly afterwards, to reappear a few minutes before Wanda, who trailed downstairs, declaring that she hadn't slept a wink and demanding to be taken to the shops without delay.

'I'm glad she's gone,' declared Pauline sorrowfully, and burst into tears.

'Hush now, love,' said Florina, 'things are never as bad as they seem.' Then she offered the making of cakes, so that the child cheered up, and presently was laughing with Florina.

Lunch dealt with, Florina changed into a dress and went through the village to see her father. She had paid him a hurried visit soon after they had got back from Holland but, despite her gifts of tobacco and whisky, he had been morose. When she went up the familiar path and opened the door, she saw that today's visit wasn't going to be a success, either. It was with relief that she went back to Wheel House, got back into her overall and apron, and went to work on the dinner.

She knew everyone who came that evening. They glimpsed her as they passed the short passage to the kitchen, and called her a good evening, and after the meal they came to the patio door to tell her what a splendid meal it had been, and ask her how she did it. It didn't seem quite the right thing but, since Sir William was with them and evinced no sign of annoyance, she supposed that he didn't mind. Presently Nanny took coffee into the drawing-room, and then went upstairs to see if Pauline was asleep, while Florina got their own meal.

They didn't linger over it. It was Sunday the next day, and there would be no help from the village and there was the picnic to prepare in the morning. They did their chores, turned out the lights and went to their beds.

Sir William had said that he would drive Wanda back after tea. Florina did her chores and then sat for a while on the patio with Nanny, drinking their coffee in the sun and watching the swans. They had an early lunch and, with Nanny comfortably resting on her bed, Florina got tea ready. Sir William had suggested that they might have it on the patio, since the Meggisons and their three children would return with them. She set out cakes and sandwiches, scones, jam and cream on the kitchen table, then covered the lot with damp cloths, and went to her room to do her hair and tidy. There would still be time to sit in the garden for an hour and leaf through the Sunday papers.

As things were to turn out, there wasn't. The picnic party returned early, making over-bright conversation, while the children looked mutinous. Florina's heart sank when she saw Sir William's face, smoothed of all expression and covering, she had no doubt, a well-bottled-up rage. She had known the Meggisons for years; she greeted them now and led the children away to wash their hands, while Wanda, looking sulky, led Mrs Meggison upstairs.

Back again, with the children milling round her, Florina took another look at Sir William. He was talking to Ralph Meggison, but he turned to her as she went out on the patio.

'Wanda had a headache,' he told her, in a voice which gave nothing away. 'I'm afraid we've cut your afternoon short.'

Florina gave her head a small shake. 'Tea is quite ready—would you like it now?'

'As soon as we are all here...'

'If Miss Fortesque's headache is bad, would the children like to have tea in the kitchen?'

'That's a very good idea. Could you bear the noise?'

'I shall like it,' she said, and meant it.

The children helped to take some of the food out to the patio, and Pauline took a tea tray up to Nanny before they gathered round the kitchen table to fall upon the food, making a great noise and laughing immoderately.

Florina laughed with them, and saw that they minded their manners and had a good tea. Finally, when they were finished, the eldest Meggison child said, 'Gosh, this is fun! We'd have hated being out there with her.'

'And who is her?' asked Florina. 'The cat's mother?'

They fell about laughing. It was Pauline who whispered, 'Wanda, of course. She grumbled all the while—it was too hot and there were wasps and the grass was damp and the food was all wrong...'

Florina bristled. 'Wrong? What was wrong? I put in everything I thought would make a picnic lunch.'

'It was super,' they hastened to reassure her. 'We ate everything. Only she was cross all the time.'

The youngest Meggison added, in a piping voice, 'She's not a country lady, not like you, Florina. You know where the mushrooms are and the blackberries and nuts. Pauline says you're going to have a dog and a cat...'

They were all shouting out suitable names to each other when Sir William joined them.

He pulled up a chair, stretched out a hand for a cake and observed, 'You *are* having fun! I've been thinking, Pauline. You had better come up to London next weekend. There's an animal sanctuary I know of—we should be able to find something suitable.' He added, as an afterthought, 'Florina, you had better come, too. I'll come down on Friday evening and we can drive back early on Saturday morning. I'll bring you and the animals back here on Sunday.'

Pauline flung herself at him, shrieking with joy. Florina, sitting sedately in her chair, would have liked to do the same. She would have the chance to see his home in London, get a glimpse of his other life, too! She looked up and caught his eye. 'Nanny will be all alone,' she pointed out.

'Mrs Deakin will sleep here. You'll need an overnight bag, that's all.' He took another cake, munched slowly and said, 'I must leave in half an hour.'

He got up, hugged Pauline, nodded to the other children, then smiled a sudden, tender smile at Florina and wandered back to the patio, leaving Florina with a red face, which was viewed with interest by her companions.

'You're very red,' said the youngest Meggison. 'Why?'

Pauline rushed to her rescue. 'It's all the cooking she does. She had to make all the food for the picnic and our tea...'

'Why didn't you come with us on our picnic?' persisted the tiresome child.

Florina had recovered her calm. 'Well, if I had, you wouldn't have had any tea. Now, if you've all finished, do you want to feed the swans? I expect you will have to go home soon.'

They all scampered away, and presently the entire Meggison family put their heads round the door to say goodbye. The youngest Meggison's parting protest that Florina should have gone to the picnic, too, left her feeling awkward, since it was uttered in piercing tones which Sir William and Wanda must have heard.

Before he left, Sir William came into the kitchen. Nanny was sitting at the table stringing beans, and Florina was at the sink peeling potatoes. He kissed Nanny on a cheek and looked across at Florina.

'Thank you for making the weekend pleasant. I'll be down on Friday as soon as I can manage.'

Her sedate, 'Very well, Sir William,' was at variance with her flushed cheeks, and he stared at her for a long moment before turning on his heel and going out to the car.

Wanda was already in it. Florina could hear her complaining voice and his mild reply as he drove away, pursued by Pauline's shrieking goodbyes.

Friday seemed an age away, but, in fact, the days went quickly. Pauline changed her mind a dozen times as to what she would wear in London, a problem Florina didn't have. If it stayed fine, she would be able to wear her pink outfit that she had bought for the trip to Holland, if it turned wet and chilly it would have to be the rather worthy suit she had had for several years.

When she got up on Friday morning the first thing she did was to hang out of the window and study the sky. It showed all the signs of a splendid day and she heaved a great sigh, for she would be able to wear the pink suit. But, to be on the safe side, she would take the jersey dress and a mac.

Sir William arrived soon after tea, and when Florina offered to make a fresh pot she was rewarded, as he sat down at the kitchen table with Pauline beside him, listening to her excited chatter and eating the buns left over from their own tea. He had given her a casual greeting, kissed Nanny who had come bustling to meet him, and presently declared that he needed some exercise and would take Pauline off for a walk. This was a good thing for Florina's peace of mind; just the sight of him had sent all thoughts of cooking out of her head. She applied herself to that now and, punctual to the minute, dished up an elegant dinner which Pauline shared along with him.

In the evening, after Pauline had gone to bed, he went along to his study, and only emerged just as she was about to go to bed, in order to remind her that they would be leaving at nine o'clock, and could they have breakfast an hour before that? His goodnight was casual, rather as though he had forgotten her. It was like looking at someone through a glass window; you could see them but you couldn't get at them, as it were.

There was a good deal of traffic on the road in the morning, but most of it was leaving London, not going into it. The Bentley sped silently up the motorway with Pauline talking non-stop and Florina sitting in the back in a contented haze of happiness, for was she not to spend the next two days in Sir William's house? Probably she wouldn't see much of him, but it was his home... She had worried at first, in case Wanda would be there too, but Pauline had asked her father and he had observed that she was spending the weekend with friends, which meant that Florina could sit back and dream about the weekend. She came awake when they stopped for coffee, joined in the talk without hearing more than half of it, and then climbed back into the car to continue her dreams, hardly noticing when Sir William slowed as they reached the outskirts of London. But gradually she became aware that he had turned away from the main streets and was threading his way through a quieter part of the city, its streets lined with tall Regency houses facing narrow railinged gardens in their centres.

The traffic here was sparse, and mostly private cars. She wasn't sure where they were, but it looked very pleasant. If one could live in such streets, she reflected, then life in London might be quite bearable.

Sir William had turned out of one street into another very similar, and stopped the car half-way along a row of narrow houses, their bow windows glistening in the sun, their front doors pristine with new paint. He got out, as Pauline skipped out on her side and ran up the short flight of steps to the door of the house before them. He opened Florina's door and ushered her out, too.

By the time they had joined Pauline at the door, Jolly had opened it, received Sir William's greeting with dignity, Pauline's delighted outburst with scarcely concealed pleasure and Florina's composed good morning with an almost avuncular mien, before standing aside to admit them.

The lobby opened out into a semicircular hall, with a graceful staircase at one side and several doors leading out of it. Sir William flung one open now and urged Florina to enter. The room was at the back of the house overlooking a small, but delightfully planned garden.

'I use this room when I'm here alone,' he explained. 'The drawing-room is upstairs, and a bit too grand unless I have guests.'

Florina, taking in the elegant furnishings, the portraits on the walls and the generously draped brocade curtains, found the room delightful but grand enough. She wondered what the drawing-room would be like. This room had a pleasant air of homeliness about it. She sat down at his request, drank the coffee Mrs Jolly brought in and, having done so, got to her feet when Pauline suggested that she should show her her room before they had lunch.

They mounted the stairs behind Mrs Jolly, and Florina was shown into a room at the head of the stairs: a beautiful room, all pink and white, with its own bathroom and a view of the street below.

'I'm next door,' Pauline explained. 'Come and see my room when you're ready.'

Warned by Mrs Jolly that lunch would be in fifteen minutes, Florina wasted five of them inspecting her room. It was really a dream, the kind of room any girl would wish for. She wondered who had furnished it right down to the last tablet of soap and matching bath oil. There was even shampoo and hand lotion, all matching. She did her face and tidied her hair, and then knocked on Pauline's door.

Her room was as pretty as Florina's, but here the furnishings were in a pale apricot, and the bed and dressing-table were painted white.

'Do you like your room?' asked Pauline eagerly. 'Daddy let me help him furnish some of the bedrooms. Of course, Wanda doesn't like them. She told Daddy that she was going to do the whole house over.'

'A pity,' observed Florina in a neutral voice. 'I find them delightful, but people have different tastes.'

They went back to the sitting-room and Florina was given a sherry before they crossed the hall to the dining-room. Its walls were papered in a rich red, the mahogany gleaming with polish. Florina, good cook that she was, could find nothing wrong with the shrimp patties, the lamb cooked with rosemary and the fresh fruit salad and cream which followed them.

They had their coffee at the table and, as they were finishing it, Sir William said, 'We will go tomorrow morning and choose a dog and cat. This afternoon I thought perhaps we might go to a matinée: I've tickets for *Cats* which starts at three o'clock. I have some telephone calls to make, then we'll take Florina round the house, shall we, Pauline?'

Florina went to bed that night in a haze of happiness; the day had been perfect, never to be forgotten. They had explored the house at a leisurely pace, allowing her plenty of time to admire everything. It was perfect, she thought, and she said so, forgetting that Wanda was going to change the lovely old furniture and the chintzes and velvets. Afterwards, they had gone to the theatre, and then to tea at the Ritz and finally back home, to sit by the window overlooking the garden, arguing happily about names for the animals.

They would leave at half-past nine the next morning, Sir William had said at dinner. 'For I have to go to the hospital and check on a couple of patients.'

After dinner, when Pauline had gone to bed, Florina sat opposite him, listening to him talking about his work. He had paused briefly to ask, 'Am I boring you? Wanda dislikes hearing about illness, but I think that you are interested.'

She had told him fervently that she was and, being a sensible girl, never hesitated to stop him so that he might explain something she hadn't understood.

She could have stayed there all night listening to him talking, but remembered in time that she was the cook, however pleasant he was being. So she made rather a muddled retreat in a flurry of goodnights and thanks, and Sir William's eyes had gleamed with amusement. He had made the muddle worse by bending to kiss her as she reached the door, so that just for a moment she forgot that she was the cook.

CHAPTER SIX

THEY spent almost two hours in the animal sanctuary. Finally, they left with an ecstatic Pauline sitting on the back seat with a large woolly dog beside her, and a mother cat and her kitten in a basket on her lap. The dog was half-grown, his ancestry so numerous that it was impossible to classify him, but he had an honest face and eyes which shone with gratitude and anxious affection. His coat was curly, and once he had recovered his full health and strength its brown colour would be glossy. He had been found by a hiker tied to a tree and left to starve. The cat and kitten had been picked up on a motorway, tied in a plastic bag. They were black and white, the pair of them, and still timid, not believing their luck.

Florina, sitting beside Sir William, listened to the child talking to her new pets and spoke her thoughts aloud. 'Isn't it nice to hear Pauline happy?'

Sir William threw her a quick sideways look. 'Is she not always happy?'

'Almost always.'

'But she is sometimes unhappy. Will you tell me why?'

'No, I can't tell you that—at least I can, but I don't choose to do so.' She added hastily, 'I don't mean to be rude, Sir William.'

His grunt could have meant anything. Presently he broke his silence. 'I shall be away for the whole of next week, and I think it likely that I shall remain in town over the weekend. Nanny will be with you, of course, but you can always phone if you need anything—Jolly will know where I am.'

She said meekly, 'Yes, Sir William,' and wondered where he would be going. To stay with Wanda? Very likely. She sat silent, brooding about it.

Back at the house, Pauline ran off to the kitchen to show Mrs Jolly her pets, and Sir William excused himself on the grounds of telephone calls to make and departed to his study, which left Florina standing in the hall, not sure what to do. It was Jolly who entered the hall just then and told her that lunch would be in half an hour, and if she cared to go into the drawing-room she would find drinks on the table under the window.

So she went in there and sat down in one of the smaller of the easy chairs. She didn't pour herself a drink, and she was surprised at Jolly mentioning it. After all, she should really be in the kitchen...

The house was quiet. But from the closed door leading to the kitchen came the sound of Pauline's excited voice. The study door was shut, so Florina nipped smartly out of the room, and crossed the hall silently. The dining-room door was half-open; she peeped round it—the table was set for three persons. She took a soft step forward and was brought to a startled halt by Sir William, speaking within inches of her ear. 'Set your mind at rest, Florina, you are lunching with us.'

She had whizzed round to gape up at his amused face. 'How did you know? I mean, I expected to eat with the Jollys,' she added fiercely. 'You forget that I work for you, Sir William.'

'Yes, I do,' he agreed, 'but for quite different reasons than those you are supposing.' He turned her smartly around. 'Shall we have a drink? We shall have to leave soon after lunch—I've a date for this evening. I'll not be down at the weekend, as I've told you already. I've a long-standing invitation I most particularly wish to keep.'

She said nothing to this. It would be with Wanda, of course; even when she wasn't there she made her presence felt, tearing Florina's futile daydreams to shreds. She sat down in the chair she had just vacated, and sipped her sherry while Sir William began a rather one-sided conversation. It was a relief when Pauline came to join them.

'The pets are having their dinner,' she explained. 'Daddy, what shall we call them?'

Names were discussed at some length during lunch. Presently, they all got into the Bentley to drive back to Wheel House, Pauline in the back with the animals and Florina beside Sir William. It would be polite to talk a little, she reflected, so she ventured a few remarks about the pleasures of the weekend and was answered in such a vague fashion that she soon gave up. Perhaps he didn't like chatter as he drove, although Pauline never stopped talking when she sat with him and he hadn't seemed to mind.

She was taken by surprise when he said, 'Don't stop talking. You have a gentle voice, very soothing. It helps me to think.'

She glanced at his profile. He was looking severe but, when he looked at her, suddenly his smile wasn't in the least severe. She began to talk about the garden and the swans and the delight of the mill stream running under the house, rambling on, speaking her thoughts aloud.

When they reached Wheel House she slipped away to the kitchen after Nanny's brief greeting, and carried in the tray set ready. Then she went to her room and put her things away. By the time she went downstairs tea was almost over, and Sir William was preparing to leave. She bade him a quiet goodbye and he nodded casually. 'Think up some of your super menus, will you? I'll be back with Wanda the weekend after next.'

'I'll look forward to that,' she told herself silently.

The two weeks went quickly, what with walking the dog, and initiating the cat and her kitten into the life of comfort they were undoubtedly going to lead. Pauline had chosen their names—Mother and Child—for, as she pointed out to Florina, that's what they were. The dog she called Bobby, because she found he answered to that name. Florina taught her to whistle, and the dog, while not looking particularly intelligent, was obedient and devoted to her. The days were placid, and even her father's ill humour couldn't spoil Florina's content. True, her thoughts dwelt overlong upon Sir William, and any titbit of news about him when he telephoned Pauline she listened to, and stored away to mull over when she had gone to bed. It was a good thing that towards the end of the fortnight she had to begin in earnest on the week-end's food. She helped around the house too, and made sure that Pauline's school uniform was ready for the autumn term was almost upon them.

Nanny, usually so brisk, looked dejected. 'They'll be married, mark my words,' she observed to Florina, as they sat together after Pauline had gone up to bed. 'The child will be at school, and next term she'll find herself a boarder there, with that woman persuading Sir William that it is just what Pauline longs for. Then it will be me, packed off, away from here. And take it from me, Florina, you won't be long following me! She won't risk having you in the house. You're young—and a nice girl—not pretty, but there is more to a girl than a handsome face . . .'

Florina murmured a reassurance she didn't feel. Being young and nice was no help at all against Wanda's cherished good looks.

Sir William arrived in time for a late tea. Florina heard the car draw up and shut the door upon the sound of Wanda's voice, strident with ill temper, raised in complaint as she came into the house.

She heard her say to Nanny, who had gone into the hall, 'Still here, Nanny? There can't be anything for you to do—according to Sir William that cook of his is quite capable of running the place. You must be longing to retire again.'

It augured ill for the weekend and Florina, warming the teapot, wished it over. The less she saw of Sir William, the better for her peace of mind. Even so, she longed to see him. She made the tea, put the tea cosy over the pot and began to butter scones.

'Well, well!' Sir William's quiet voice took her by surprise. 'My own kitchen door shut against me! Pauline has been commandeered to help Wanda unpack.' He took a scone and ate it with relish. 'And how are you, Florina?'

He studied her face carefully, and she reddened under his gaze. 'Very well, thank you, Sir William.'

He began on another scone. 'Jolly is with us. Will you or Nanny see that he is comfortable? He has driven down in a Mini—you can drive? You'll be able to take Pauline to school and fetch her.'

She said faintly, 'Oh, will I?' and passed the plate of scones, since he seemed bent on eating the lot.

'There aren't all that number of people I would trust to drive her. Could you escape from the stove tomorrow morning—before breakfast? We'll go for a run?'

All her resolutions about keeping out of his way disappeared like smoke. 'It's breakfast at half-past eight . . .'

'Couldn't be better. Seven o'clock be OK?' He didn't wait for her answer, but took another scone and wandered out of the kitchen, leaving her door open.

Which meant that after a few moments she heard Wanda's voice as she came downstairs. She was still complaining and Nanny, coming for the tea tray, had a face like a thunder cloud. 'In a fine temper, she is—wanted to stop at some posh hotel for tea, but Sir William wanted to come straight home.'

She stalked off with the tray and Florina set the table for their own tea, helped by Jolly, who had just come into the house.

It was a pleasant meal, with Jolly and Nanny keeping the conversation carefully to generalities. This was a disappointment to Florina, who had hoped to glean news about Sir William and Wanda. After tea, there was no time to talk. There was dinner to see to which kept her in the kitchen for several hours, aware that Pauline's voice, raised and tearful, interlarded by Bobby's bark and Wanda's regrettably shrill tones, were hardly contributing to a happy evening.

Mother and Child were curled up cosily before the Aga, presently to be joined by a furious Pauline and Bobby, who, being good-natured himself, expected everyone else to be the same.

'I hate her!' declared Pauline. 'If Daddy marries her, me and Bobby will run away. She said he smelled nasty.' She sniffed, 'Daddy said it was time for his supper, and then him and me—I—will take him for his walk.'

Daddy seemed good at pouring oil on troubled waters. Florina watched Pauline feeding the animals. The child was entirely engrossed in this, and happy, but how soon would her happiness be shattered once Wanda had become her stepmother? Sir William, much as she loved him, had been remarkably mistaken in his choice of a second wife. Men, thought Florina, however clever, could be remarkably dim at times.

She was in the kitchen all the evening, so that she saw neither Sir William nor Wanda. It was bedtime by the time they had eaten their own supper and cleared it away. Since Jolly had undertaken to remain up until Sir William retired himself, she and Nanny said goodnight and went to their respective rooms.

It was one o'clock in the morning when Florina woke on the thought that she had forgotten to put the porridge oats to soak. Nanny was a firm believer in porridge, but it had to be said that she insisted it was made according to her recipe—old-fashioned and time-consuming. She got out of bed, without stopping to put on a dressing-gown and slippers, and nipped down to the kitchen. There would be no one around at that hour. She put the exact amount of oats into water in a double saucepan, added the pinch of salt Nanny insisted upon, and stirred it smoothly before filling the steamer with hot water and setting the whole upon the Aga. Having done which, she stepped back and glanced at the clock, and then let out a startled yelp as Sir William, speaking from the door where he had been lounging watching her, observed, 'Such devotion to duty! It's one o'clock in the morning, Florina.'

She curled her toes into the rug before the stove and longed for her dressing-gown. 'Yes—well, you see I forgot the porridge. Nanny likes it made in a certain way, and I forgot to soak it. I'm very sorry if I disturbed you . . .'

He said gravely, 'Oh, you disturb me, but you have no need to be sorry about it.' He stood looking at her for a long moment, and when he spoke his voice was very gentle. 'Go to bed, my dear.'

She flew away without a word, intent on escape, wishing with all her heart that she *was* his dear. Sleep escaped her for the next hour or so, so that the night was short, but she got up and dressed and plaited her hair neatly at the usual time. Then she went down to the kitchen, intent on making tea before they set out, thankful that it would give her something to do, for, remembering their early-morning meeting, she was stiff with shyness.

Sir William was already there, with the tea made and poured into mugs. His good morning was casually friendly, and he scarcely looked at her, so she calmed down and, by the time they reached the garage, she was almost her usual calm self.

Sir William was hardly the build for a Mini. Florina, despite the smallness of her person, found it a tight fit with the pair of them. To make more room he had flung an arm along the back of the seat and she was very aware of it; nevertheless, she made herself concentrate on her driving, going along the narrow country road to Wilton and then back on the main Salisbury road, and taking the turning to the village, over the bridge opposite the farm.

'Quite happy about ferrying Pauline to and fro?' he asked as she ran the little car into the garage. He got out, strolling beside her towards the kitchen door.

'If Pauline's up we'll take Bobby for a walk.' He turned on his heel and then stopped and turned around to face her. 'You have such beautiful hair—a shining mouse curtain. You should wear it loose always.

'It would get in the soup,' said Florina.

Wanda came downstairs mid-morning, beautifully dressed and made-up, ready to be entertained. It was a pity that everyone should be in the kitchen with the door to the patio open, milling around, drinking coffee, feeding the swans from the patio, playing with the cats and brushing Bobby. In the middle of this cheerful hubbub, Florina stood at the table making a batch of rolls, quite undisturbed by it all. Nobody else noticed Wanda's entrance, and Florina paused long enough to say politely, 'Good morning, Miss Fortesque. Would you like coffee?'

Sir William looked up briefly from Bobby's grooming. 'Hello, Wanda, Pauline and I are going to her school to see her headmistress—like to come with us?'

Wanda shuddered delicately. 'Certainly not. I can't sleep in this house. I'll rest on the patio, if someone takes that dog away. Cook, you can bring me some coffee once I'm settled.'

Sir William said quietly 'Jolly will do that. Come on, Pauline, we'll be off.' He whistled to Bobby, remarked that they would be back for lunch, and disappeared in the direction of the garage.

Wanda needed a lot of settling: fresh coffee, more cushions, a light rug, the novel she had left in her bedroom. Nanny, looking more and more po-faced, handed these over wordlessly and then disappeared, and so presently did Jolly, leaving Florina to take the rolls from the oven and then start on lunch.

She was arranging cold salmon artistically on a bed of cress and cucumber, when Wanda called her. It would have given Florina great satisfaction to have ignored her, but Wanda was a guest and, what was more, a cherished one. And Florina, in a mixed-up, miserable way, would have done anything to make Sir William happy, even if it meant being nice to Wanda. She washed her hands well and went on to the patio, prepared to offer cool drinks, more cushions or anything else the girl demanded.

She was completely taken aback when Wanda said, 'Don't think I haven't eyes in my head. I've watched you toadying to Sir William—God knows what crazy ideas you've got in that silly head. I dare say you fancy you are in love with him. Well, you can forget it. The day we marry, and that shall not be too far away, you'll get your notice, so you had better start looking for another job.'

Florina, usually so mild, seethed with a splendid rage. She said in a very quiet voice, 'You have no right to talk to me like this. When Sir William tells me to leave, then I shall go, but not one minute before. I think that you are a rude, spoiled young woman, who has no love or thought for anyone. You don't deserve to be happy, but then, you never will be...' She put her neat head on one side and studied the other girl, who was staring speechlessly at her. 'You may report all that I've said to Sir William, but I wish to be there just in case you forget what you said to me, too.'

'If it's the last thing I do,' breathed Wanda, 'I'll see you pay for this.' She sat up and caught Florina a smart slap.

'Cool off, Miss Fortesque.' Florina, who hadn't realised that she could feel so royally angry, picked up the jug of lemonade on the table by Wanda's chair, and poured it slowly over the top of her head. The rather syrupy stuff caused havoc to Wanda's artlessly arranged hair, and did even more damage to her complexion. She jumped to her feet, shrieking threats as she raced away to her room, and Florina put down the jug and went back to the salmon. She had cooked her goose, but just for a moment she didn't care.

Jolly was in the kitchen. He eyed her with a benign smile and a good deal of respect. 'I saw and heard everything, Miss Florina. If necessary I will substantiate anything you may need to say to Sir William. I was prepared to come to your assistance, but it proved unnecessary.'

The enormity of what she had done was permeating through her like an unexpected heavy fall of rain. 'Oh, Mr Jolly, thank you. You're very kind. It was very wrong of me and I forgot that I was just the cook. She'll have me sacked.'

'I believe that you may set your mind at rest on that score,' observed Jolly, who had had several interesting chats with Nanny and was totally in agreement with her. Florina would be a splendid wife for Sir William—and she was in love with him—although she was unaware of how much that showed. As for Sir William, he was old enough and wise enough to get himself out of the mess he had so carelessly let himself get into. Jolly had no doubt that he would do it in his own good time, and when it suited him, and with such skill that Miss Fortesque would believe that she had been the one to call their marriage off. In the meantime, Jolly made a mental note to call Florina 'Miss Florina'—it would be a step in the right direction.

There was no sign of Wanda until lunch time, a meal she ate in a haughty silence which Sir William didn't appear to notice. When they had finished she said in an unnaturally quiet voice, 'William, I must talk to you—now.'

Jolly conveyed this news to the kitchen and Florina, hearing it, lost her appetite completely. Indeed, she was feeling quite sick by the time they had finished, and when Sir William strolled in, she went so white that the freckles sprinkling her nose stood out darkly.

He crossed to the Aga, stooped so as to stroke Mother and Child curled together in a neat ball, and said in his placid way, 'I'd like a word with Florina, if you wouldn't mind...'

Florina watched Jolly and Nanny go through the door, put her hands on the back of the chair she was standing behind and met Sir William's gaze.

'Miss Fortesque has told me a most extraordinary tale—have you anything to add, Florina?' His voice was kind.

'No.'

'There are always two sides to a disagreement. I should like to hear yours.'

'No.'

He smiled a little. He studied the nails of one hand. 'Pauline was listening at the study door, and indeed Miss Fortesque was speaking so loudly, I was forced to send her to her room so that she could indulge her mirth.'

'Please don't ask me to apologise. I'm not the least sorry for what I did. I expect you're going to give me notice.'

He looked surprised. 'Why should I do that? I had hoped that you knew me well enough to tell me your version, but it seems that it is not so.'

Florina burst out, 'How can I tell you? You are going to marry Miss Fortesque.'

He smiled again. 'That is your reason?' And, when she nodded, 'I think that it might be better to say no more about the matter.' He started for the door and paused to look back at her. 'It seems that lemonade plays havoc with tinted hair.'

Jolly was in the hall, so obviously waiting for him that Sir William said, 'Come into the study, Jolly. I take it that you wish to speak to me?'

Jolly closed the door behind him. 'I was in the kitchen, Sir William, and, begging your pardon, Miss Fortesque was that nasty—Miss Florina was so polite too, in the face of all the nasty rubbish . . .'

'Rubbish, Jolly?'

Jolly, who had an excellent memory, repeated what had been said. He noticed with satisfaction that Sir William's face had no expression upon it, which meant that he was concealing strong feelings. He wisely added nothing more.

Sir William was silent for several moments. 'Thank you, Jolly. You did right to tell me. I have told Florina that the matter is to be forgotten.'

'Very good, Sir William. Miss Florina is a nice young lady and easily hurt.'

'Quite so.' He smiled suddenly, and looked young and faintly wicked. 'Will you go to Pauline's room and ask her if she wants to take Bobby and me for a walk? Miss Fortesque is resting in her room, but I dare say she'll be down for tea.'

The rest of the weekend passed off peacefully. Florina kept to her kitchen and tried to expunge her bad behaviour by cooking mouth-watering meals and keeping out of the way of Sir William and Wanda. Pauline, when she wasn't with her father, spent her time in the kitchen, with Bobby in close attendance, curled up before the Aga with the cats.

'Wanda is so cross, I'd rather be here with you,' she explained. 'Daddy said I wasn't to talk about it, but I laughed and laughed. But she is horrid—I shall run away...'

'Now, love, don't talk like that. It would break your father's heart if you were to leave him. He loves you so much.'

'So why is he going to marry Wanda? He doesn't love her.'

'You mustn't say that, she is a a very lovely lady.'

'With a black heart,' declared Pauline, so fiercely that they both laughed.

The house seemed very empty when the Bentley had gone the next day. Sir William had bade Florina a casual goodbye, kissed Pauline and Nanny, swept Wanda into the front seat before there was time for her to say anything, ushered Jolly into the back of the car and driven off. He hadn't said anything about the following weekend. Perhaps he would stay in town to placate Wanda, take her dining and dancing, so that she could wear her lovely clothes and show off the enormous ring she wore on her engagement finger.

Florina retired to the kitchen and got supper, with a good deal of unnecessary clashing of saucepans.

There was plenty to keep her busy during the next few days: tomato chutney to make, vegetables from the garden to blanch and pack into the freezer, and she had Pauline to keep her company when she wasn't having her sewing and knitting lessons with Nanny, something the old lady insisted upon. It was quite late on Thursday evening when Florina heard a car turn into the drive and a moment later the front door shutting. She went down the passage into the hall and

Sir William was there. He was standing in the centre of the lovely old Persian carpet, staring at the wall, but he turned to look at her. He was tired; his face had lines in it she hadn't seen before.

She said at once, 'You'd like something to eat—I'll have it ready in ten minutes. Shall I pour you a drink?' She shook her head in a motherly fashion. 'You've had a very busy day.'

He gave a short sigh and then smiled at her. 'Pour me a whisky, will you? Will Pauline be awake?'

She glanced at the clock. 'Probably not, but she would love you to wake her up.'

She watched him going upstairs two at a time, and then went into the drawing-room to switch on a lamp or two and pour out his whisky. The room looked lovely in the soft light, and the gentle flow of the mill stream under the floor was soothing. She hurried back to the kitchen, to warm up soup. An omelette would be quick, and there were mushrooms she could use. She was laying a tray when he came in, the glass in his hand. 'I'll have it here—anything will do...' He sat down at the table and watched her whisking the eggs. 'I should have telephoned you. I'm examining students at Bristol tomorrow, and on Monday and Tuesday. I'll drive up each day—I don't need to be there until ten o'clock and I can be back here in the early evening.'

Florina poured the soup into a pitkin and set it before him. Her heart sang with delight at the prospect of him being at Wheel House. She said happily, 'Oh, now nice—to have you here...' She paused and then went on quickly, 'Nice for all of us.

Since he was staring at her rather hard, the spoon in his hand, she added, 'Do eat your soup, Sir William, and I'll make your omelette. There's bread and butter on the table. Would you like coffee now or later?'

'Now, if you will have it with me.'

She got two mugs and filled them from the pot on the Aga, put one before him and then went back to the frying-pan, where the mushrooms were sizzling gently. He began to talk, going over his week and, although for half the time she had very little idea of what he was talking about, she listened with interest, dishing up the omelette and then watching him eat it while she drank her coffee. This was how it should be, she reflected: someone waiting for him each evening to share his day's work with him and see that he ate a proper meal and could talk without interruption . . .

'Of course, you won't understand half of what I'm saying,' observed Sir William and passed his mug for more coffee.

'Well, no—I wish I did! I can understand why you love your work. I think that I would have liked to have been a nurse and to have known a bit more about all the things that you have been talking about. I'm too old to start training now, though.'

'Old?'

'I'm twenty-seven, Sir William.'

'I'm thirty-nine, Florina.' He leaned back in his chair. 'Is there any of that jam you made last week?'

She fetched it, put the loaf and a dish of butter on the table and watched him demolish a slice. When he had finished, she said matter-of-factly, 'You should go to bed, Sir William. When will you be leaving in the morning?'

'Eight o'clock.'

'Will breakfast at half-past seven suit you, or would you like it earlier?'

'That will do very well. I'll help you with these things. You should be in bed yourself.'

He ignored her refusal of help, but found a tea-cloth and dried the dishes as she washed them. He waited as she saw to the animals and climbed the stairs to her room, and then went back to the hall. But he didn't go at once to his bed, he went into the drawing-room and sat down in his great chair, deep in thought. Presently he got to his feet, stretched hugely, turned off the lights and went upstairs. His thoughts must have been pleasant ones, for he was chuckling as he went.

Florina was dishing up the breakfast when he came into the kitchen with Pauline, dressing-gowned and bare-footed, so she did a second lot of bacon and eggs and, much as she would have liked to have stayed, took herself off on the plea of giving Bobby a quick run in the garden. She didn't go back until she judged Sir William would be ready to leave, but he was still sitting at the table. There was a faint frown on his face, and Pauline's lower lip was thrust out in an ominous fashion. He got up as Florina came in, kissed his daughter, whispered in her ear—something which made her small face brighten—observed that he would be back around six o'clock and went to the patio door, fending off Bobby's efforts to go with him, and passing Florina as he went. His swift kiss took her by surprise, and he had gone before she could do more than gasp.

'Why did Daddy kiss you?' Pauline wanted to know. 'Perhaps it was because Wanda wasn't here—though she doesn't like being kissed. She says it spoils her make-up.'

The child stared at Florina. 'You haven't got anything on your face, have you, Florina? You are awfully red . . .'

The days went too quickly. The brief glimpses she had of Sir William in the morning coloured her whole day, and in the evenings once he was home, even though he saw little of her, she could hear him talking to Pauline, calling the dog, chattering with Nanny. Once dinner was over and the house was quiet, she listened to his quiet footfall crossing the hall to the study and gently closing the door. She pictured him sitting at his desk, making notes or correcting papers. He might just as easily be writing to Wanda or talking to her on the telephone, but she tried not to think of that.

Tuesday came too soon. He left after breakfast and didn't intend to come back until the weekend, for he would drive straight back to London from Bristol. He mentioned casually, as he went, that probably he would be bringing Miss Fortesque with him at the weekend.

Pauline cried when he had gone, climbing on to Florina's lap and sobbing into her shoulder. 'Do you suppose they'll be married?' she asked.

'Most unlikely,' said Florina bracingly. 'Your father would never do that without telling you, love. So cheer up and wash your face. We'll take Bobby for a nice walk, and when we get back you can go into the garden for a bit and keep an eye on Mother and Child, in case they stray off.'

She had reassured the child, but not herself. She had long ago discovered that Sir William was not a man to display his feelings, or, for that matter, disclose his plans. He was quite capable of doing exactly what he wished, without disclosing either the one or the other, and Wanda was a very attractive girl. Florina went and had a look at herself in the small looking-glass in the downstairs cloakroom and derived no comfort from that. The quicker she erased Sir William from her thoughts, the better. It would help, of course, if she could find a substitute for him, but she had known all the young men in the village since she was a small girl, and they had either got engaged or married or had left home. She didn't know anyone... She did, though. Felix, the only young man to show any interest in her, and one she had no wish ever to meet again.

She went to get Nanny's breakfast tray ready, reflecting that the chances of seeing Felix again were so remote that she need not give him another thought.

CHAPTER SEVEN

FLORINA took Pauline and Bobby for short trips in the car during the next few days, and even Nanny consented to be driven into Wilton for an afternoon's shopping. Summer was giving way slowly to the first breath of autumn, and there weren't many days left before Pauline would be going to school. The three of them made the most of it, and it wasn't until Friday morning, when Sir William telephoned, that they remembered that Wanda would be with him that weekend. Reluctantly, Nanny prepared the rooms while Florina bent her mind to the menus for the next few days. She was rolling pastry for the vol-au-vents when she heard a car stop in the drive. Her heart gave a great leap—perhaps Sir William had come early, and, better still, Wanda might not be with him. She heard Nanny go to the door and the murmur of voices, and then Nanny came into the kitchen.

'Someone for you—a young man—says he is an old friend.' She looked at Florina's floury hands. 'I'll put him in the small sitting-room.'

Florina frowned. 'But I haven't any old friends—not young men...' She remembered Felix, then raised a worried face to Nanny. 'Oh, if it's Felix—I don't want to see him, Nanny.' She added by way of explanation, 'He's from Holland. I met him when I went over there for the wedding.'

'Well, if he's come all this way, you can't refuse to see him. It's only good manners,' declared Nanny, a stickler for doing the right thing.

She went away before Florina could think of any more excuses. Florina finished rolling her pastry, put it in the fridge to keep cool and washed her hands. She didn't bother to look in the looking-glass; her face was flushed from her cooking and her hair, still in its plait, could have done with a comb. But if it *was* Felix, and something told her that it was, then she had no wish to improve her looks for him. She would give him short shrift, she decided crossly as she opened the sitting-room door.

It *was* Felix, debonair and very sure of himself. He came across the room to meet her, just as though they were good friends with a fondness for each other. But she ignored his outstretched hands and said crisply, 'Hello, Felix. I'm afraid I have no time to talk, I've too much to do. Are you on your way somewhere? Tante Minna didn't mention you in her letter.'

'I didn't tell her. I'm putting up at the Trout and Feathers; I thought you could do with a bit of livening up. I've got the car, we can drive around, go dancing, hit a few of the night-spots.'

'You must be out of your mind! I work here, it's a full-time job, and when I'm free I don't want to go dancing or anything else, especially with you, Felix. I can't think why you came.'

'Let's say I don't like being thwarted.' He smiled widely, and she thought that his eyes seemed closer together than she had remembered.

'I don't know what you mean . . .' They had been speaking Dutch, but now she switched to English. 'You are wasting your time here, Felix. I have neither the time nor the inclination to go out with you, even if it were possible.'

He shrugged his shoulders. 'I've taken the room for a week. There's no reason why I shouldn't spend it here if I wish.'

'None at all, but please don't come bothering me. Now, you will have to excuse me, I'm busy.'

'No coffee? Where's your Dutch hospitality?'

'I'm not in a position to offer that, Felix. I'm cook here.'

She led the way through the hall and opened the door. On the threshold, he paused. 'Just a minute. Doesn't your father live here?'

'Yes, he does, but he has no interest in Mother's side of the family—not since she died.'

'Ah, well, they will know where he lives if I ask at the pub.'

He gave her a mocking salute and got into his car.

She shut the door slowly and found Nanny in the hall beside her. The old lady's stern features were relaxed into a look of concern, so that Florina found herself pouring out a rather muddled account of her meeting with Felix at Tante Minna's house, and her dislike of him. 'I thought I'd been unfair to him,' she explained, 'for he was very nice at the wedding. It was afterwards . . .'

Nanny nodded. 'A conceited young man, and not a very pleasant one,' she commented. 'Did Sir William meet him?'

'Yes.' Florina went pink, for undoubtedly he thought that she and Felix were rather more than firm friends, even though she had denied it. What was he going to think if Felix came to see her? And he was quite capable of it . . .

She went back to the kitchen and finished the pastry. She was so worried that she curdled the *béarnaise* sauce, which meant that she had to add iced water, a teaspoon at a time, and beat like mad until it was smooth again.

Preparations for the evening's dinner dealt with, she and Pauline took Bobby for his walk. She expected to meet Felix at every corner, but there was no sign of him. Perhaps he had realised that there was no chance of seeing much of her, and had driven off somewhere where there was more entertainment. She was able to wish Sir William a rather colourless good evening when he arrived, and was relieved to hear Wanda go straight upstairs without bothering to say anything to anyone.

'And how is the village?' enquired Sir William. 'Anything exciting happened since I was last here?'

'Nothing—nothing at all,' said Florina, so quickly that he took a long look at her. Guilt was written all over her nice little face, but he forebore from pursuing the matter. Instead, he sighed inwardly; she was holding something back, and until she had learned to trust him utterly there was little he could do about it. He made some casual remark about Mother and Child sitting as usual before the Aga, then strolled away. He could, of course, question Nanny, but he dismissed the idea at once. Florina would have to tell him herself. Until she trusted him he couldn't be sure...

It was after breakfast the next morning that Felix walked up the drive, rang the bell, and demanded of Nanny, who had answered to door, to see Sir William. He was charming about it, but very determined, and she had no choice but to put him in the small sitting-room and tell Sir William.

So this was Florina's secret, he reflected, shaking hands with Felix, good manners masking his dislike.

'This is a surprise,' he observed. 'You are on holiday?'

Felix gave him a look of well simulated surprise. 'Oh, hasn't Florina told you? I'm staying in the village for a week—so that we can see something of each other. I thought that she would be free for part of each day so that we could be together...'

Sir William said mildly, 'I'm afraid that she doesn't get a great deal of time to herself, especially at the weekends. If you had warned her before you came, something could have been arranged. Perhaps she can manage a half-day after the weekend.'

He got to his feet and Felix, perforce, got to his. 'So sorry,' Sir William said. 'You'll forgive me, I'm sure. I have a guest and have the morning planned.'

He bade Felix goodbye at the door and remained there until he was out of sight, then he shut the door quietly and went along to the kitchen.

Florina was peeling potatoes at the sink, lulled into a sense of false security, so that the enquiring face she turned towards him was serene. But it took only a few seconds for her to realise that something was wrong.

Sir William wandered over to the table and sat on it. 'Your friend Felix has just called to see me. Why didn't you tell me he was in the village, Florina?'

She plunged at once into a muddled speech. 'I don't want to—that is he came yesterday—I didn't think——' She made matters worse by adding, 'I didn't have time to talk to him...'

'But you had time to tell me. Remember? I asked you if there was any news and you said—I quote, "Nothing—nothing at all." Why so secretive, Florina? Did you think that I might not allow my cook to have followers?'

'He's not a follower,' she mumbled.

'He followed you here. I think I'm entitled to...' He fell silent as the door opened and Pauline came in, Bobby in her arms.

'Daddy, Wanda is still in bed. Could we go for a walk until she gets up? There's a darling little calf at the farm. Florina and I went to look at it and we can go any time we like, so I don't suppose they'll mind you, instead.'

She looked at Florina's pale, strained face and then at her father.

'Are you quarrelling?' she wanted to know.

Sir William put a hand on her small shoulders and went to the door.

'When you are old and wise enough, darling, you will understand that one never quarrels with one's cook.' He sounded savage.

Florina finished the potatoes and started scraping carrots. She felt numb and her head was quite empty of thought. Presently, the whole of the little scene came flooding back, and her eyes filled with tears so that she could hardly see what she was doing. Finally, indignation swallowed up every other feeling. He hadn't given her a chance to explain, he had taken it for granted that the wretched Felix actually meant something to her, and he had been unkind, more than that, utterly beastly. It would serve him right if she were to spend an evening with Felix...

She finished the carrots and started on the salsify, and when Nanny came into the kitchen presently, she left the sink and poured coffee for them both.

Nanny sipped appreciatively. 'You make very good coffee, child.' She glanced at Florina's pink nose. 'What's upset Sir William, I wonder? In a nasty old temper when he left the house. Not that any that didn't know him well would even guess at it, but I've known him since he was a baby!'

She took another quick peep at Florina. 'Had all his plans laid, I dare say, and someone's messed them up. Did I see that young man coming up the drive an hour or so ago? I wonder what he wanted? A trouble-maker if ever I saw one.'

Florina said, 'He came to see if I could go out with him. I imagine that he let Sir William think that I knew he was coming to stay.' She poured more coffee. 'Nanny, I'd rather not talk about it, if you don't mind.'

Nanny nodded. 'Least said . . .' She didn't finish because Wanda came into the kitchen. 'Oh, there you are—this is the worst run household I've ever had to endure. I want coffee in the drawing-room. I won't wait for Sir William.' She turned on her heel and then paused. 'Who was that young man who called earlier this morning? Rather good-looking, I thought. Why haven't I met him before? Does he come from the village—he looked a cut above that.'

Nanny was silent, so was Florina.

'Well, who was he?' She laughed suddenly. 'Never your boyfriend, Cook? I find that hard to believe.' Her laugh became a snigger. 'It was!' She watched Florina's face glow. 'What a joke! Are you the best he can manage? Does Sir William know?' And, when no one answered, 'Yes, he does. I wonder what he thought of it? His marvellous cook with a boyfriend up her sleeve. Well you'll be free to marry him, if that is what he wants, won't you? For you won't be here much longer, I promise you that.'

She swept out of the kitchen, leaving the two of them silent. Presently Nanny said, 'You did quite right not to say anything.' Her sharp eyes searched Florina's pale face. 'She will use this to her advantage—urge Sir William to let you go, so that you can get married...'

Florina nodded miserably. 'But Nanny, I don't want to marry him—even if he were the last man left on earth.'

'I know that. Is he serious about you?'

Florina shook her head. 'I didn't respond and he expected me to. He got very angry...'

'A nasty type. You had better tell Sir William. He'll see that he doesn't bother you again.'

Florina said quite violently. 'No—no, I don't want to talk about it to him. Please don't say anything to him, Nanny. Promise?'

Nanny said briefly, 'I'll promise, if it will make you happy, though you're making a big mistake.' She wouldn't break her promise, but if she could see a way round that she would take it. If there was a misunderstanding at this stage it would be a great pity. Here was Florina, bless the girl, head over heels in love with Sir William and making no effort to do anything about it because cooks didn't marry their employers, especially when they were wealthy and at the top of their profession. And Sir William already engaged to that awful Miss Fortesque... and he as uncertain as a young man in the throes of his first love affair. Nanny, incurably romantic under her severe exterior, sighed deeply, refused more coffee and went away to tidy the chaos in Wanda's bedroom, bearing a tray of coffee for that lady as she went.

Florina stayed in the kitchen, bent on keeping out of sight. She was putting the finished touches to a trifle when Pauline and Bobby joined her. 'Daddy wants his coffee. I said I'd take it. We had a lovely walk and Bobby ran for miles.'

She peered into Florina's face. 'Darling Florina, you look so sad. Was Daddy angry with you?'

Florina arranged the tray and put a plate of little almond biscuits beside the coffee-pot. 'Good gracious, no, love! I'm not a bit sad, only rather headachy. Go carefully with the tray. Shall I put another cup on it, for you?'

'May I have my milk here with you? Wanda told Daddy that she wanted to speak to him seriously. She's being all charming and smiling—I bet she's up to no good . . .'

Florina agreed silently, although she said firmly, 'Pauline, you mustn't say things like that about your father's guests. It would hurt his feelings.'

Pauline picked up the tray. She said, with the frankness of children, 'But he hasn't any feelings for her, I can tell; he's always so polite to her. I can't think why he's going to marry her.'

'People marry because they love each other.'

Pauline kissed her cheek. 'Dear Florina, you're such a darling, but not always quite with it.' She took a biscuit and munched it. 'If Daddy was poor and just Mr Sedley, she wouldn't want to marry him. She worked on him—you know—all sweet interest and how clever he is and all that rubbish. I suppose he thought she'd make quite a good stepmother for me, and he just let himself be conned.' She kissed Florina again, picked up the tray and skipped off before Florina's shocked rebuke could reach her ears.

She was back quickly. 'Daddy's angry! His face is all calm and his eyes are almost shut. I couldn't hear what Wanda was saying but her voice sounded as though she was in church. You know, all hushed and very solemn.'

Florina muttered something neither hushed nor solemn, and said rather loudly, 'I expect they are discussing their wedding.'

Pauline drank some of her milk and, since Florina wasn't looking, poured some of it into Mother's saucer. 'No, they weren't, because I listened a teeny bit as I was closing the door and she said, "Let's have him for drinks, darling."'

Florina dropped the wooden spoon she was holding and took a long time to pick it up.

'Someone from the village, I expect,' she said, knowing in her heart that it was Felix. Well, if it was, she would keep out of sight. She would be busy with dinner, anyway.

It wasn't until after tea that Nanny came to tell her that someone was coming for drinks. 'Sir William didn't say who it was.' She caught sight of Florina's face. 'That young man . . . this is Wanda's doing. She can be very persuasive when she wants; probably painted a pathetic picture of you pining for his company. Did you see very much of him in Holland? And did Sir William see you together?'

Florina nodded dumbly. 'I wish I could run away!'

'Run away? Unthinkable! Besides you're not the girl I think you are if you do. Must I still keep my promise?'

Florina lifted a stubborn chin. 'Yes, please.' She added hopefully, 'Probably he won't come in here. He'll be a guest, after all, and only a casual caller . . .'

It was worse than anything she could have imagined. She was piping creamed potatoes on to a baking tray when the door opened and Sir William, Wanda and Felix came into the kitchen.

It was Wanda who spoke. 'Oh, Cook—here is Felix.' She paused to give him a conspiratorial look.

'You don't mind if I call you that?' She smiled at Florina with eyes like flints. 'He can't wait to talk to you. You are such a marvellous cook that I'm sure it won't bother you if he stays while you work for a while?'

Florina looked at her and then at Felix, grinning at seeing her cornered. Lastly, she looked at Sir William. He was leaning against the door, apparently only mildly interested. She said in a high voice which she managed to keep steady, 'I'm sorry, I can't work in this kitchen unless I'm alone.'

'In that case,' said Sir William, 'let us leave you alone, in peace. I don't want my dinner spoilt.'

Wanda didn't give up easily. 'Pauline is always here...'

He said mildly, 'Certainly she is, but she helps Florina, fetching and carrying, washing up and generally making herself quite useful. And I entirely approve, I should like her to be as good a cook as Florina. I doubt if—er—Felix wishes to wash the dishes.' He turned politely to him. 'You must have another drink before you go. I'm sure we shall be able to arrange something at a more propitious time.'

The party left the kitchen, leaving her shaking with temper. She attacked the food she was preparing quite savagely, curdling a sauce and burning the *croûtons*. With the kitchen full of blue smoke and the pungent smell of the charred remains at the foot of the pan, she clashed lids, dropped spoons and spilt some clarifying butter on to the floor.

It was to this scene of chaos that Sir William returned.

'Something is burning,' he observed.

'I know that!' she snapped. 'Dinner is ruined.' An exaggeration, but excusable in the circumstances.

His fine mouth twitched. 'I'm sorry that we upset you by coming into the kitchen. Wanda was sure that you would be delighted, and certainly there was no need for you to be so reluctant to mention it to me . . .'

'Reluctant? Reluctant?' said Florina shrilly. 'And pray why should I be that? In any case, it's my business, Sir William.' Rage sat strangely upon her, her eyes blazed in her usually tranquil face, her soft mouth shook. Sir William eyed her very thoughtfully.

'This Felix,' he said at last. 'Are you in love with him?' When she remained silent, he went on, 'No, don't tell me again that it's not my business. After all, it's my dinner which is ruined. But you're not going to tell me, are you, Florina? I wonder why that is?'

She spoke in a small whispering voice. 'You made up your mind that I was being deceitful about him, you—you said he was my follower—that was to remind me that I was your cook, so if you don't mind I will not tell you anything, Sir William. I will make sure that he doesn't come here again. I'm sorry if it has embarrassed you.'

'Good God, girl, why should it do that? On the contrary, it enlightened me.' He was going to say more, but the door was pushed open with an impatient hand, and Wanda came in. She was wearing a white crêpe dress and her hair was carefully arranged in careless curls; she looked sweet and feminine and most appealing.

'William, I'm so glad you are here, now you can hear me say how sorry I am to Cook. I embarrassed her, but I truly thought she would be pleased.' Her blue eyes swam with tears, as she turned to Florina. 'You must think I'm quite horrid. Don't bear a grudge against me, will you? I told Felix that I was sure that you would have time to see something of him while he is here. After all, you won't have anything much to do once we are gone.'

She tucked a hand under Sir William's arm, and smiled at him prettily. 'Don't be cross with me, darling, for giving orders in your house. After all, it's soon to be mine as well, isn't it?'

Sir William said nothing to that, only stared at Florina. 'We'll go,' he said briskly. 'Florina has had enough interruptions.'

Alone once more, Florina set about rescuing the dinner from disaster. 'Not that I care if everything is burnt to a cinder,' she said to Mother. 'Anyway, you and Child can have the egg custard—it's not fit to put on the table.'

Sir William made no attempt to seek her out. Indeed, it seemed to her that he was avoiding her. Usually he came into the kitchen with Pauline in the morning while she fed Bobby and the cats, sitting astride a chair, talking to Florina about the village and telling her his plans for the garden, but not any more. Nor, to her relief, did she see anything of Felix. Sunday came and went, there were friends for drinks, and very soon after lunch he drove back to London with Wanda, smiling a small, triumphant smile, sitting beside him. He had bidden Florina goodbye in a pleasant manner, but the easy friendship between them had gone.

She got through the rest of the day somehow, presenting a bright face to Pauline and Nanny, and presently retiring to bed to weep silently for the impossible dreams which would never return. At least she had derived a spurious happiness from them.

It was several days later when Pauline came dancing into the kitchen to tell her that her father wanted to speak to her. Florina lifted the receiver with the air of one expecting it to bite her and said a cautious "hello".

Sir William's firm voice was crisp. 'Florina? Jolly will drive Mrs Jolly down tomorrow. They will arrive some time after lunch and he will return here after having tea with you. Mrs Jolly will take over from you for two days so that you may be completely free, so make any arrangements you like with Felix; he told me that he wouldn't be returning until Saturday morning.' He added, in a strangely expressionless voice, 'I hope you will have a pleasant time together.'

He had rung off before she could do more than let out a gasp of surprise. Florina toyed with the idea of ringing him back and denying all wish to see Felix again, but that might make matters worse. She detected Wanda's hand in the business and flounced off in search of Nanny.

That lady heard her out. 'Dear, dear, here's a pretty kettle of fish. Does Felix know about this?'

'I don't know, I shouldn't think so—I'm sure Sir William wouldn't phone him deliberately, just to tell him.'

'Miss Fortesque might,' suggested Nanny. 'You must think of something, so that if he comes round here you are ready for him.' Her stern face broke into a smile. 'I have it! Isn't Pauline to spend the next day or so with the Meggisons? You know them, don't you? Could you not go with her? Heaven knows, they have more than enough room for you in that house of theirs.'

'Yes, but what would I say? I can't just invite myself.'

'You can tell them the truth, the bare bones of it, at any rate. If that man comes, don't say anything about it, but get hold of Mrs Meggison and go there with Pauline—she's to get there early after breakfast, isn't she? He is not likely to call as early as that. Don't worry about him, I'll deal with the gentleman.'

'Won't Jolly tell Sir William?'

'Bless you, child, he'll not breathe a word...'

'I'm deceiving Sir William...'

'He's been deceiving himself for months,' observed Nanny cryptically. 'You can tell him when he comes at the weekend.'

Felix arrived later that day and Florina, bolstered by the knowledge that Nanny was on the landing, listening, admitted him into the hall, but no further.

'So, Miss Fortesque kept her promise. She said she would persuade Sir William to give you a couple of days off. I'll be round for you tomorrow about eleven o'clock, and don't try any tricks. Everyone knows in the village that we are going to be married.' He chuckled at her look of outrage. 'Don't worry, darling, I'll be off and away at the end of the week, but I don't like being snubbed by a plain-faced girl who can't say boo to a goose. I'm just getting my own back.' He made her a mock salute. 'Be seeing you! I've planned a very interesting day for us both.'

She shut the door on him and then locked it. They had spoken in Dutch and Nanny, descending the stairs, had to have it all translated.

'Conceited jackanapes!' she declared. 'Who does he think he is? Why, he's nothing but a great lout under all that charm. Now, off you go and ring Mrs Meggison, and make sure you'll be collected well before ten o'clock.'

'Yes, but what about Pauline? Won't she think it's strange?'

'Why should she? She knows that the Meggisons are old friends of yours, and she loves being with you.'

Mrs Meggison raised no objections, in fact, she was delighted. 'I have to go to the dentist in the morning and I was wondering what to do about the children—now you will be here to keep an eye on them. It couldn't be better, my dear. Can you stay until Saturday? We'll send you both back directly after breakfast if Sir William doesn't mind.'

'He won't mind at all,' said Florina mendaciously, and put down the receiver with a great sigh of relief.

The Meggisons were genuinely pleased to see her. 'You can't think how glad I am that you came,' declared Mrs Meggison. 'There's a new au pair girl coming next week—Danish—and the boys go back to school then, but with all four of them at home I've been run off my feet. Cook and Meg have enough to do; I can't ask them to keep an eye on the children as well. They are all in the garden. Perhaps Pauline would like to trot out and be with them while I show you your rooms.'

It was a nice old house; a little shabby, but the furniture was old and cared for and the rooms held all the warmth of a happy family life. Florina, safely away from Felix's unwanted attentions, enjoyed every minute of their two days, even though she had almost no time to herself. There was so much to do. The school holidays were almost over and they wanted to extract the last ounce of pleasure from them. They worked wonders for Pauline, too, tearing around, climbing trees, riding the elderly donkey the Meggisons kept in the orchard, eating out-of-doors in the untidy garden at the back of the house. The pair of them, much refreshed, climbed into Mr Meggison's Land Rover with mixed feelings. Pauline sorry to be leaving her friends, but anxious to see Bobby and Mother and Child again. Florina was relieved that Felix would be gone, but panicky about meeting Sir William. She hadn't told Pauline to say nothing about her stay with the Meggisons; she had been deceitful, but she didn't intend that the little girl should be involved, too. For deceit it was, whichever way she looked at it. She got out of the Land Rover when they reached Wheel House, mentally braced against meeting Sir William.

Jolly opened the door, beaming a welcome, and invited Mr Meggison to make himself at home in the drawing-room while he sent for Sir William.

'In the kitchen garden, sir, and if Pauline would go and fetch him . . .'

Pauline went, dancing away, shrieking with delight as Jolly went on smoothly, 'Mrs Jolly is in the kitchen, Miss Florina—there'll be coffee there and I have no doubt she will wish to have a chat with you. We return to London later this morning, but Sir William and Miss Fortesque are here for the weekend.'

Florina had her coffee and a comfortable chat with Mrs Jolly, and then went to her room to change her clothes; there had been no sign of Sir William, and Miss Fortesque had been driven into Salisbury by Jolly directly after breakfast to have her hair done. Mrs Jolly had cleared the kitchen, but since Jolly and she were driving back to London before lunch, Florina would prepare it.

It was almost two hours later, while she was mixing a salad with one eye on the clock, anxious not to be late with the meal, when Sir William strolled into the kitchen.

'I believe we should have a talk,' he observed, at his most placid.

'Oh, yes, of course, Sir William, but lunch will be late...'

She had gone pale, but she didn't avoid his eyes.

'Never mind lunch! You had two days free so that you might spend them with Felix, instead of which, you chose to go to the Meggisons. Why?'

He had taken one of the Windsor chairs by the Aga, and Mother and Child had lost no time in clambering on to his knee. He stroked them with a large, gentle hand and waited for her to answer.

She said coldly, 'I don't know why you should suppose that I should want to spend my leisure with Felix. I didn't ask him to come here in the first place and, as far as I know, I gave you no reason to suppose that I did.'

She sliced tomatoes briskly, ruining most of them because her hand wasn't steady on the knife.

'You didn't make that clear, and I still wonder why. Am I not to know, Florina?'

She was making a hash of a cucumber. The salad wouldn't be fit to eat.

'No, Sir William. I'm sorry I didn't tell you that I was going to the Meggisons, but I didn't think it would matter...'

'On the contrary, it matters very much, but that's something we need not go into for the moment. So I take it that you have no plans to marry?'

'No.'

He set the cats back in their basket, got to his feet and wandered to the door. 'Good, Pauline will be so pleased. You should be more careful in the future, Florina. I've been quite concerned about you.'

He went away, closing the door quietly behind him, leaving her to start on another salad, which would be fit to put on the table.

She was feeding the swans after lunch was finished, when Wanda came on to the patio. Sir William and Pauline had taken Bobby for a walk, and the house was quiet, Mrs Deakin had gone and Nanny was in her room resting.

'I don't know what game you're playing, Cook,' Wanda's voice was soft and angry. 'Whatever it is, it won't do you any good. By next weekend we shall announce the date of the wedding, and don't think it will be months ahead. Sir William will get a special licence and we can marry within days. You had better start looking for another job.' She sniggered. 'You are a fool! You and your silly daydreams, did you suppose that a man like Sir William would look at you twice? When he does look at you he is looking at his cook, my dear, not you. You had better go back to your Dutch family and find yourself a husband there—you haven't much chance here, even with the village men.' She turned away. 'Don't say that I haven't warned you. You will not stay a day longer than is necessary once I have married Sir William.'

Florina stood where she was, staring down at the water below and the family of swans gobbling up the bread she was throwing to them still. It was something to do while she tried to collect her thoughts.

That Wanda was going to get rid of her was a certainty, and to go to Holland was surely a way out of a situation which was fast becoming unbearable. On the other hand, she would be running away and, as Nanny said, she wasn't a girl to do that. Would there by any point in remaining in England? It wasn't as if she would see Sir William again.

She threw the last crust and watched the swans demolish it. She couldn't see them very clearly for the tears she was struggling to hold back.

'Why are you crying?' asked Sir William and, since she didn't answer, threw an arm round her shoulders and stared down at the swans, too.

CHAPTER EIGHT

THE urge to put her head on Sir William's vast chest and tell him everything, even that she loved him, was something Florina only prevented herself from doing by the greatest effort. Instead, she sniffed, blew her small red nose and stayed obstinately silent.

Sir William sounded calmly friendly. 'Your father—he lives close by, does he not? Would you like to spend a day or two with him? He could probably dispel the rumours Felix has spread.'

'It's kind of you to suggest it Sir William, but Father and I... he wanted a son, and he has no interest in the Dutch side of me. He tried to turn Mother into an Englishwoman, but he never succeeded—he didn't succeed with me, either.' Her voice was small and thin.

Sir William, who had heard that before from various sources in the village, said comfortably, 'Well, what would you like to do, Florina? You haven't been happy since we came back from Holland, have you? Did something happen then to upset you—and I don't mean Felix?' He added, 'Would it help if you went back there for a week or two? Not to your aunt, for Felix goes there, does he not? I have some good friends in the Hague and Amsterdam; and in Friesland, too—a temporary job, perhaps?'

She was very conscious of his arm on her shoulders. Did he want to be rid of her, in order to placate Wanda and at the same time to spare her from the ignominy of getting the sack? She didn't know, and did it really matter? she reflected.

'I hope you will stay with us.' He had answered her unspoken thoughts so promptly that for a moment she wondered if she had voiced them out loud. 'At least until Pauline is settled in her new school. Will you think about it for a week or so?'

He gave her a comforting pat on the arm, remarking that he had to work in his study, and he left her there.

They exchanged barely a dozen words before he left for London, and as for Wanda, she behaved as though Florina wasn't there; she ignored Nanny, too, and avoided Pauline, but hung on to Sir William's arm on every possible occasion, the very picture of a compliant, adoring wife-to-be.

They wouldn't be down on the following weekend, Sir William told his daughter; he had a consultation on Saturday in Suffolk and he might possibly need to spend the night there. 'I'll phone you each evening,' he promised, 'and you can tell me all about school.'

The week went quickly but now there was another routine, no longer the easy-going times of the holidays, but up early, school uniform to get into, breakfast and then the drive to Wilton, with Bobby on the back seat of the car. It was Florina who took him off for his walks now during the day, although when Pauline got home each afternoon the three of them went into the fields around the village while Pauline recited the happenings of her day to Florina. She was at least happy at school; she knew some of the girls there and the teachers were nice. She had homework to do, of course, and Florina sat at the kitchen table with her and helped when she was asked, while Nanny sat by the Aga, knitting. It was pleasant and peaceful, but Florina worried that it wasn't the life Pauline should have. She needed a mother; her father loved her but he had his work and she suspected that without Wanda he would have more time to spend with his daughter. When Wanda was his wife, that didn't mean that she was going to be Pauline's mother; indeed, with herself and Nanny out of the way, the child would be packed off to boarding-school. Wanda wasn't the kind of woman to share her husband, even with his own child.

The weekend came and since the weather was still fine, the Meggisons came over for tea on Saturday and played croquet on the velvet-smooth lawn behind the house, until Florina called them in for supper and presently drove them back home in the Mini, very squashed with Bobby insisting on coming, too.

When Florina went to say goodnight to Pauline, the child flung her arms round her neck. 'Such a lovely day,' she said sleepily. 'If only Daddy could have been here too.'

'That would have been nice,' agreed Florina sedately, and her heart danced against her ribs at the thought. 'But he said he'd be home here on Friday.'

It was, however, sooner than Friday when she saw him again.

It was on Tuesday morning, while they were driving along the country road to Wilton, that a car, driven much too fast, overtook them on a bend to crash head on into a Land Rover coming towards it.

Florina pulled into the ditch by the roadside; the two cars were a hundred yards ahead of her, askew across the road, the drivers already climbing out, shouting at each other. Pauline had clutched her arm when the cars had collided and then covered her ears from the thumps and bangs of the impact.

Florina opened her door a few inches. 'I'll go and see if they can move out of the way; if they can't we'll have to go round along the main road.' She glanced at Bobby, barking his head off and shivering. 'Don't get out, darling, and don't let Bobby out; he's very frightened and he'll run away.'

She nipped out of the car smartly and shut the door against the terrified dog, and ran up the road.

No one was hurt, only furiously angry. The two men were hurling abuse at each other until she took advantage of a pause in their vituperation.

'Am I able to get past you?' She had to shout to make them listen. 'I'm taking Pauline to school...' She had recognised one of the farm hands from the village, standing by the Land Rover. 'Will you be able to move soon?'

'Now, luv, that I can't say—this lunatic was coming too fast—you must have seen him—we'll have to get the police and take numbers and the rest. You'd best go round, and back over the bridge.'

There seemed nothing else to do, and Florina turned to go back to the Mini in time to see the door open and Pauline get out. Bobby scrambled out after her, and then, yelping madly, raced away through a gap in the hedge, into the fields beyond. Within seconds Pauline had gone after him, climbing the five-barred gate in the hedge. She took no notice of Florina's shout, just as Bobby took no notice of the child's cries.

Florina reached the car, snatched up the dog's lead, slammed the door shut and climbed the gate in her turn. The men were still arguing, she could hear them even at that distance, much too taken up with their own problems to bother about hers. Bobby was well away by now, running erratically across a further field, newly ploughed, and Pauline wasn't too far behind him. Florina saved her breath and ran as she had never run before. She knew the country around her well;

beyond the ploughed field was a small wood, its heavy undergrowth overgrown with rough scrub and brambles, and beyond that was the river winding its way into Wilton, not isolated but unproductive so that not even gypsies went near it.

Bobby had reached the wood, but Pauline was finding the ploughed field heavy-going. However, she didn't stop when Florina shouted, so she had reached the wood before Florina was half-way there.

The wood was quiet when she reached it, save for the birds and the frenzied distant barking of Bobby. There was neither sight nor sound of Pauline; she was probably on the far side by now, making for the river.

The brambles made speed impossible if she weren't to be scratched to pieces, but scratches were the least of her worries. The wood ran down steeply to the river, which, while not wide or deep, was swift-running and, at this time of the year, cluttered with weeds and reeds; Pauline might rush along without looking and fall into it. Bobby was still yelping and barking and she was sure that she heard Pauline's voice; it spurred her on through thc brambles, quite regardless of the thorns.

The wood was narrow at that point, and she emerged finally, oozing blood from the scratches which covered her hands and arms and legs. Her dress was torn, as were her tights, and her hair hopelessly tangled, hung in an untidy curtain down her back. She swept it out of her eyes and paused to look around her. Bobby was whining now, but there was no sign of Pauline. She shouted at the top of her voice and started down the steep slope to the river. There were willows and bushes along its banks; she found the child within inches of the water, lying white and silent with Bobby beside her. He greeted her with a joyful bark, bent to lick the little girl's face, and made no effort to run away as she fastened his lead before kneeling beside Pauline.

There was a bruise on Pauline's forehead and a few beads of blood. Florina, her heart thumping with fear, picked up a flaccid hand and felt for a pulse. It was steady and quite strong, so she put the hand down and began to search for other injuries. There were plenty of scratches but, as far as she could tell, no broken bones. She made Pauline as comfortable as she could, tied Bobby's lead to a nearby tree-stump, and tried to decide what to do. She glanced at her watch; it was barely half an hour since they had started their mad race across the fields. She thought it unlikely that either man would have noticed it, for they had been far too occupied with their argument. Pauline was concussed, she thought, but even if she regained consciousness, she didn't dare to let the child walk back to the car; it must be the best part of a mile away. She could only hope that the farm worker would tell someone when he got back to the village, better still, he might go to the police station. This hope was instantly squashed; there was no room to turn on that particular stretch of the road, and they would have to manhandle the car to one side so that the Land Rover could squeeze past. In the village the police could be informed and someone sent to take the car away; it had received by far the most damage.

She sat down by Pauline and lifted the child's head very gently on to her lap. They might be there for hours; even if the men noticed that the Mini was standing there and no one was in it, they might have thought that they had walked back to the village.

Which was exactly what they had thought; it was almost half an hour before they had got the car on to the side of the road and the Land Rover proceeded on its way, and it was pure chance that the driver saw Nanny walking down the road to get some eggs from the farm. 'They'll be back now,' he observed. 'I didn't pass them on the road.'

'But they aren't here. Did you see them get out of the car? They weren't hurt?'

'No, luv, but that little old dog was kicking up a fine row, ran off, he did, though lord knows where.' He started the engine. 'They'll turn up, safe and sound, but I'll tell the police—we'll have to go to the station in Wilton, and they'll come out here, I've no doubt of that.'

Nanny went on her way to the farm, collected the eggs, and marched back to Wheel House. There was no sign of Florina or Pauline, so she phoned the school; there was always the chance that they had walked the rest of the way...

They hadn't, and when she phoned the police at Wilton they had no news of them. They would ring back, they told her, the moment they knew anything; they couldn't have gone far...

It was a pity that an elderly woman living half a mile along the road from the accident should declare that she had heard a dog barking behind her cottage, on the opposite side of the road to where Bobby had escaped; she thought, too, that she had seen someone running. She was vague and uncertain as to exactly when she had seen them and the excitement of being the centre of interest for the moment led her to embroider her talk, so that the two policemen who had been detailed to search for Florina and Pauline set off in the opposite direction to the wood and the river.

Sir William wasn't in when Nanny telephoned his house, but Jolly undertook to track him down and tell him. 'He'll be at the hospital,' he told her, 'but he's not operating, he mentioned that at breakfast and he said that he had a quiet morning—just ward rounds. He will be with you in a couple of hours.'

It was less than that; Sir William spent ten precious minutes ringing the police, aware that if he warned them he would be allowed to travel at maximum speed provided they had his car number and he gave his reasons.

The Bentley made short work of the ninety miles, and he walked into his house to find Nanny on the telephone. She said 'Thank you,' and put the receiver down as he reached her. 'Thank God you've come, Sir William, I'm that worried!' She studied his face. He looked much as usual, but he was pale and there was a muscle twitching in his cheek. 'You'll have a cup of coffee,' and when he held up a hand, 'You can drink it while I tell you all that I know.'

She was upset, but very sensible too—time enough to give way to tears when they were safe and sound. Sir William listened and drank his coffee and observed, 'The police have drawn a blank so far in Wilton and the direction of Broad Chalke; I'll try the other side, it's open country, isn't it? Where exactly did the accident happen?'

'The Land Rover driver said on the sharp bend about two miles along the road, almost parallel with that road you can see on the left . . .'

Florina, with Pauline's head heavy on her lap, glanced at the sky; the clouds were piling up and although it was barely one o'clock, there was a faint chill heralding the still distant evening. Pauline had stirred a little, but she hadn't dared to move. Bobby, quite quiet now, sat beside her, aware that something was wrong, fidgeting a little. She had shouted for a time, but there had been no answer and the trees in the wood deadened the sound of any traffic on the distant road. She had racked her brains to find a way to get them out of the fix, but she could think of nothing. It was unlikely that anyone would come that way, for there was no reason to do so, and who would take a country walk through brambles, anyway, but it surprised her a little that no one had searched for them; they weren't all that far away from the scene of the accident.

Pauline stirred again and this time she opened her eyes. 'Florina?' she stared up in a puzzled way. 'I've got such a fearful headache.'

'Yes, darling, I expect you have. You fell over and you bumped your head. Don't move or it will hurt still more. As soon as someone comes, we'll have you home and tucked up in bed.'

'Bobby—where is Bobby?'

'Right here, beside me. Now close your eyes, my love, and have a nap; I'll wake you when someone comes...'

'Daddy will find us.'

Florina said stoutly, 'Of course he will,' and blinked away a tear. She was thoroughly scared by now, as much by her inability to think of a way of getting back through the wood, as by the fact that no one had come within shouting distance.

It was at that precise moment that someone did shout, and for a few seconds she was too surprised to answer. But Bobby set up a joyful barking and began to tug at his lead. Florina shouted, then set him free and watched him tear up the bank and into the wood, to emerge a few moments later with Sir William hard on his heels.

She was beyond words, she could only stare at him as he came to a halt beside her and squatted down on his heels. He let out a great sigh and said, 'Oh, my dears . . .' and his arm drew her close for a moment before he bent to examine Pauline.

She stirred under his gentle hand and opened her eyes. 'Daddy—oh, I knew you'd come, Florina said you would. Can we go home now?'

'Yes, darling, but just me take a look and see where you're hurt.'

Florina found her voice. 'She was unconscious when I found her, that was half-past nine. I didn't move her, she came round about eleven o'clock.'

He nodded without looking at her. 'There doesn't seem to be much wrong except concussion. We'll get you both home and put her to bed—she had better be X-rayed, but I think it's safe to leave that until the morning.' He looked at her then. 'And you, Florina, are you hurt?'

'Only a few scratches. Will you carry her through the wood?'

'The pub landlord and Dick from the farm came with me—they are searching at either end of the wood.' He put his fingers between his teeth and whistled and presently she heard their answering whistles.

'Shall I wait for them here? I'll bring Bobby with me, then you can go ahead with Pauline.

For the first time he smiled. 'Having found you, Florina, I have no intention of leaving you again.' He watched the look of puzzlement on her face, and added, 'They will be here very soon.'

Going back was easier. The two men went ahead, beating back the brambles with their sticks, with Sir William carrying Pauline behind them and, behind him, protected by his vast size, came Florina, leading a sober Bobby on his lead.

At the roadside she made to get into the Mini, but Sir William said no. 'You will come with us, Florina. Dick had a lift here; he can drive the Mini back, if he will.' He grinned at the two men. 'We'll have a pint together later.'

He laid Pauline on the back seat, swept Florina on to the seat beside him and drove back to Wheel House.

Nanny was waiting. 'Bed for Pauline, Nanny. I'll leave her to you for a moment; she's been concussed so you know what to do. Florina, get out of those clothes, have a hot bath and come downstairs to me. I must phone the police and Pauline's school.'

He went on up the stairs with Pauline, and Florina went to her own room, undressed slowly and sank thankfully into a steaming bath. The sight of herself in the wardrobe mirror had made her gasp in horror; her hair was full of twigs and leaves, her dress was ruined and her tights were streaked with blood from scratches. She gave a slightly hysterical giggle and then fell to weeping. But the bath was soothing, and then, once more in her cotton dress and apron, her hair brushed and plaited as usual, a dusting of powder on her scratched face, she went back to the kitchen.

Sir William was there, pouring tea. 'I don't know about you,' he remarked cheerfully, 'but when I've been scared I've found that a cup of tea works wonders at restoring my nerve.'

'You've never been scared...' She gasped at him in amazement.

'Just lately, I have, on occasion, been scared to death. Come and sit down and tell me just what happened. I've told the police, and Mrs Deakin kindly called at your father's house and told him all was well.'

'I'm sorry we've been such a nuisance.' She glanced at Bobby, lying with the cats, fast asleep. 'It wasn't anyone's fault, at least, it was the man who overtook us—he was going too fast, the Land Rover couldn't do anything about it. I shouldn't have got out of the car, only both men were shouting at each other and I had to find out if anyone was hurt and if we had a chance of getting by...'

'Pauline got out with you...?'

'Oh, no, of course not, but I'm sure she was afraid, and Bobby was beside himself; he'd gone in a flash and she left after him. I'm sure she thought that she would be able to catch him easily, but the poor beast was terrified.'

Sir William picked up one of her hands from the table; it was covered in scratches and he examined them, his head bent so that she couldn't see his face. 'My poor dear...' His hand tightened on hers and it was as though an electric current had flooded her whole person. She sought to pull her hand away, but he merely tightened his grip as he lifted his head and looked at her, half smiling, his eyes half hidden beneath their heavy lids. She stared back at him, her eyes wide. It was a magic moment for her, shattered almost before she had realised it by Nanny's entrance. Sir William let her hand go without haste and asked, 'Everything all right, Nanny?' in his calm voice.

Nanny had looked at them and away again. 'The child wants to sit up and she says she's hungry.'

He got up. 'I'll go and take a good look; I don't think there's much damage done, and there's no reason why she shouldn't have a light meal, but wait until I've looked at her.'

He went away and Nanny went to the Aga to see if the kettle was boiling.

'We could all do with something,' she observed briskly. 'Do you feel up to getting a meal ready, Florina?'

Florina gave her a sweet bemused look. 'Of course, Nanny. Soup and scrambled eggs with toast and mushrooms and coffee.'

She went to get the eggs, still in a dream, unwilling to give it up for reality. For his hand on hers and his look, tender and urgent, must have been a dream: a conclusion substantiated by his return presently with the prosaic suggestion that Pauline could have both the soup and the scrambled eggs, and wouldn't it be a good idea if she and Nanny had a meal as well? As for himself, he went on, he would go to the Trout and Feathers and have a drink with the landlord and some bread and cheese.

So she shook the dreams from her head and set about getting lunch. They had finished and tidied the kitchen and Nanny had gone to sit with Pauline when Sir William returned. He came straight into the kitchen and sat down on the table. 'I'll feel easier in my mind if I take Pauline back with me; she can be X-rayed at my hospital and if there is anything amiss it can be put right. I'm almost certain that there's nothing to worry about, but I must be sure. We'll leave after breakfast; you will come with us, Florina?'

Her heart gave a great leap, so that she caught her breath.

'Very well, Sir William. Are we to stay overnight?'

'Yes, pack for two or three days, to be on the safe side. I'm going to Pauline's school now. When does Mrs Deakin come?'

'Not until tomorrow morning.'

'Then will you go and see her and ask if she will sleep here with Nanny? If she can't, perhaps Mrs Datchett would oblige us. They'll be paid, of course.'

He went to the door; stopped there to turn and look at her. 'You're all right? I'll give you something for those scratches; you've had ATS injections?'

She nodded, striving to be matter of fact. 'Oh, yes, I had a booster done about six months ago. I'll go along to Mrs Deakin now. Does Pauline know that she is going back with you?'

'No. I'll tell her when I get back. I'll have dinner here with you and Nanny—shall we say eight o'clock? That gives Nanny a chance to settle Pauline first. I'll go up and see her now before I go out.'

He nodded casually and left her there.

Mrs Deakin would be delighted to oblige; she was saving up for a new washing machine and Sir William was a generous employer. Florina skimmed back quickly, not liking to leave Nanny alone, but Nanny was sitting in the rocking chair in Pauline's room, knitting while Pauline slept. Florina made a cup of tea and took it upstairs to her, whispered about plans for the evening and took herself off back to the kitchen. There was plenty to do; a good thing, for she had to forget about Sir William. She bustled about assembling a suitable meal for him: spinach soup, lamb chops, courgettes in red wine, calabrese and devilled potatoes, with an apricot tart and cream to follow. She would have time to make the little dry biscuits he liked with his cheese; she rolled up her sleeves and started her preparations.

She took up Pauline's supper tray and sat with her while Nanny had an hour to herself. The little girl was apparently none the worse for their adventure; she ate her supper without demur and now that she was safely home and in her bed was inclined to giggle a good deal about their adventure. She submitted to Florina's sponging of her face and hands, declared herself ready to go to sleep and, when her father came quietly in, did no more than murmur sleepily at him.

He felt her head, took her pulse and pronounced himself satisfied, kissed the child and picked up the supper tray and beckoned Florina to go with him.

'I've phoned the hospital,' he told her. 'We'll leave just before eight o'clock. She can travel as she is, wrapped up in a blanket. Pack her some clothes, though.'

He was matter-of-fact—more than that, casual—and she strove to match him. They ate their dinner carrying on a guarded conversation about nothing much, and Nanny, sitting between them, watched their faces and thought hopefully of the next day or two in London, praying that Wanda wouldn't be there, and that they would have time together; that was all they needed. Sir William, she was sure now, had realised that he was in love with Florina, and as for Florina, there was no doubt in Nanny's mind where her heart lay. Things would sort themselves out, she reflected comfortably.

The journey to London was uneventful. Pauline lay on the back seat with Florina beside her, and she was content to be quiet, and Florina had her own thoughts, her eyes on the back of Sir William's handsome head.

There were people waiting for them when they reached the hospital: porters with a stretcher, Sir William's registrar, one of his housemen and the children's ward sister, young, pretty and cheerful. She said a friendly 'Hi,' to Florina, standing a little apart, not sure what was expected of her, before she accompanied the stretcher into the hospital.

It was Sir William who paused long enough to say, 'My registrar, Jack Collins, and my houseman, Colin Weekes.' He caught her by the arm. 'You might as well come along, too.'

She sat when bidden, in the X-ray Department waiting-room, for what seemed a very long time. People came and went: nurses, porters, a variety of persons bustling along as though the very existence of the hospital depended upon them, and presently Sir William strolled in, looking, she had to admit, exactly like a senior consultant should look. He was trailed by a number of people, who stood back politely as he came to a halt beside her.

'No problems,' he told her. 'A few days taking things quietly and Pauline will be quite well. I'll drive you both home now, but I must come back here for the rest of the day. The Jollys will look after you. Get Pauline to bed, will you? Don't let her read or watch television, but she can sit up a little.' He nodded. 'Ready?'

Jolly was waiting for them. Sir William carried his small daughter up the stairs to her room with Mrs Jolly and Florina hard on his heels, while Jolly fetched their bags. In no time at all, Pauline had been settled in her bed, her few clothes unpacked, and Sir William, with a murmured word to Jolly, had departed again.

Florina found herself in the same room that she had had previously, bidden by Mrs Jolly to make haste and tidy herself, and, since Pauline was a little peevish and excited, would it be a good idea if she had her lunch in the child's room? There was a small table there and perhaps Pauline would settle down and have a nice nap if someone was with her.

Which presently, was exactly what happened. Florina sat quietly where she was for a time, thinking about Sir William. She had been foolish to fall in love with him, although she could quite see that one couldn't always pick and choose whom one loved, but their worlds were so far apart, her visit to the hospital had emphasised that . . .

She picked up her tray, carried it downstairs and stayed for a few minutes in the kitchen talking to Mrs Jolly. 'You'll need a breath of air,' declared that lady. 'I'll bring you both up a nice tea presently and sit with Pauline while you have a quick walk. Sir William won't be home before six o'clock.'

'That's kind of you, Mrs Jolly; perhaps I'll do that. Pauline mustn't read or watch television. I thought I'd read aloud to her before her supper.'

She went back through the baize door into the hall just as Jolly went to answer the front door. It was Wanda, who pushed past him and then stopped dead in her tracks as she caught sight of Florina.

'What are you doing here?' she demanded. Her blue eyes narrowed. 'Up to your tricks again, are you? What a sly creature you are—the moment my back is turned.'

She had crossed the hall and was standing at the foot of the stairs so that Florina couldn't get past her without pushing.

Florina, conscious that Jolly was hovering by the baize door, kept her temper. 'Pauline had an accident; Sir William has brought her here so that she could go to the hospital for an X-ray—somebody had to come with her. She is upstairs asleep.'

Wanda didn't answer, and Florina said politely, 'I'm going upstairs to sit with her—if you wouldn't mind moving . . .'

Wanda didn't budge. She turned her head and said very rudely: 'You can go back to the kitchen, Jolly.'

But he didn't move, only glanced at Florina. She smiled and nodded to reassure him, and he went reluctantly away.

'How long are you staying here?' demanded Wanda.

'Until Pauline is well enough to go back to Wheel House. Sir William will decide...'

'Oh, Sir William, Sir William!' gibed Wanda. 'He's the top and bottom of your existence, isn't he? You're such a fool too, just because he treats you decently and appears to take an interest in you—don't you know that that is part of his work? Being kind and sympathetic—turning on the charm for hysterical mothers, listening to their silly whining about their kids.'

Florina interrupted her then. 'That is not true and it's a wicked thing to say! Sir William is kind and good and he loves his work. You can say what you like about me, but you are not going to say a word against him.'

Wanda burst out laughing. 'Oh, lord, you're so funny—if only you could see that plain face of yours.' She said suddenly, seriously, 'Do you know that we are to be married next week? Your precious Sir William didn't tell you that, did he? But why should he? You are only his cook, and not for much longer, either.'

She turned away and sauntered towards the drawing-room. 'You'd better get back upstairs and keep an eye on that child before she does something stupid.'

Florina went up the stairs without a word, shaking with rage and misery and, under those feelings, prey to first doubts. Wanda had sounded so sure of herself, and indeed, there was no reason at all why Sir William should tell her his plans. She went into Pauline's room and sat down to think, thankful that Pauline was dozing. Her head remained obstinately empty of thoughts; it was a relief when the little girl wakened and demanded to be read to. So Florina read *The Wind in the Willows*, until Pauline declared that she would like her tea.

'I'll pop down and get us a tray, love,' promised Florina. The house was quiet when she went downstairs. There was still some time before Sir William would return, perhaps she would be able to think a few sensible thoughts by then.

She was in the hall when the drawing-room door opened and Wanda came out.

'Had time to think?' she wanted to know. 'Not that it will make any difference; only a fool like you would be so stupid . . .'

The street door opened and Sir William asked quietly. 'Who is stupid?'

Florina had a cowardly impulse to turn and run back upstairs but quelled it; even Wanda had been taken by surprise. 'Wanda, I didn't expect to find you here . . .'

She shrugged that aside. 'I'll tell you who's stupid,' she said spitefully. 'Your cook.' She laughed. 'She's in love with you, William.'

He didn't look at Florina. 'Yes, I know.' He spoke gently. 'You haven't told me why you are here. Shall we go into my study while you tell me?'

He still hadn't looked at Florina, standing like a small statue, her face as stony as her person.

It was only when the door had been closed gently behind them that she moved. She went to the kitchen and fetched the tea tray, oblivious of the Jollys' concerned faces, and only when Mrs Jolly offered to sit with Pauline so that she might have an hour or two to herself did she say in a wispy voice, 'I'd rather stay with her, thank you so much, Mrs Jolly.'

She carried the tray back upstairs, saw to Pauline's wants and poured herself a cup of tea. Mrs Jolly had gone to a lot of trouble with their tea; little scones, feather-light, mouth-watering sandwiches, small iced cakes—Florina, pleading a headache in answer to Pauline's anxious enquiries as to why she didn't eat anything, plunged into talk. There was plenty to say about Bobby and the cats, and school, and whether would Nanny remember to feed the swans. Once tea was over Florina got out *The Wind in the Willows* again and began to read in her quiet voice.

She was interrupted by Sir William, who sauntered in, embraced his daughter and said in a perfectly normal voice, 'I'll sit with Pauline for a while, Florina. I dare say you would like a breath of air. I have to go out this evening, but I shall be back after dinner—I should like to talk to you then.'

She kept her eyes on his waistcoat. Her 'Very well, Sir William,' was uttered in what she hoped was a voice which showed no trace of a wobble.

She went out because she could think of nothing else to do. A nice quiet cry in her bedroom would have eased her, but if she cried her nose remained regrettably pink for hours afterwards and so did her eyelids.

She marched briskly, unheeding of her surroundings for half an hour, and then she turned round and marched back again. The exercise had brought some colour into her white face, but her insides were in turmoil. She would have given a great deal not to have to see Sir William later that evening; she could, of course, retire to bed with a migraine, only if she did he would undoubtedly feel it his duty to prescribe for her. 'Don't be a coward,' she muttered as she rang the doorbell to be admitted by a silently sympathetic Jolly. 'Sir William has just gone out, Miss Florina; he hopes to be back by nine o'clock. Dinner will be at half-past seven in the small sitting-room. Mrs Jolly would like to know if she can help in any way with Pauline.'

'We've given her a great deal of extra work as it is. I'll go up to her and settle her down before dinner. Wouldn't it be less trouble if I were to join you and Mrs Jolly?'

'Sir William's orders, Miss Florina—I dare say he thinks that after the exciting time that you've had you could do with some peace and quiet.'

Pauline was tired at any rate; she ate her supper, submitted to being washed and having a fresh nightie, and declared sleepily that she was quite ready to go to sleep. Florina kissed her goodnight, left a small table lamp burning and went away to tidy herself. She had no appetite, indeed she was feeling slightly sick at the thought of the coming interview, but she would have to wear a brave face...

She managed to swallow at least some of the delicious food Jolly put before her, and, since there was still some time before Sir William would return, she sat over her coffee, still at the table, so lost in a hotch-potch of muddled thoughts that she didn't hear Sir William's return.

When she looked up he was standing in the open doorway, watching her. She was so startled that her cup clattered into the saucer and she got clumsily to her feet, her head suddenly clear. She loved him; it didn't matter that he knew, for what difference would that make? She had felt a burning shame in the hall listening to Wanda's spite tearing her secret to shreds, but now she merely felt cold and detached, as though she was watching herself, a self who wasn't her at all.

Sir William's eyes hadn't left her face. He said, 'If you've finished your coffee, will you come to the study?'

She walked past him without a word, for really she had nothing to say. He opened the door and she went past him and sat, very straight-backed and composed in the chair he offered her.

CHAPTER NINE

SIR WILLIAM sat down in his chair behind the desk and rather disconcertingly remained silent. He sat back, unsmiling, apparently deep in thought, which gave Florina time to admire his stylish appearance. He was wearing a dinner-jacket, beautifully tailored, and a plain dress-shirt of dazzling whiteness. Dinner with Wanda, thought Florina; somewhere wildly fashionable where all the best people went. Wanda would have been tricked out in the forefront of fashion—taffeta was in fashion, preferably in a vivid colour like petunia. She frowned—definitely not a colour for Wanda—ice blue, perhaps, or black . . .

She became aware that Sir William had said something and she murmured, 'I'm sorry. . . I was thinking.'

Because he had nothing to say to that she gushed on, in terror of a silence between them. 'Wanda—Miss Fortesque, you know—she looks her best in black or that very pale blue . . .'

Behind the gravity of his face she suspected that he was laughing, but all he said was, 'Just for the moment, shall we leave her out of it?' He leaned forward and put his elbows on the desk.

'I think that you should go away for a time, Florina. You have had a tiresome few weeks.' His eyes searched her face and he went on deliberately, 'That is something which we don't need to discuss. I have a colleague at the hospital, a Dutchman over here for a seminar. He will be returning home in a couple of days' time and it so happens that the English girl who helps to look after his children is anxious to go off on holiday. It might suit you very well to take over from her for a few weeks?'

'You don't want me to be your cook?' said Florina baldly.

He smiled faintly. 'That is a difficult question to answer at the moment. The situation is such that I believe the best thing for you is to accept Doctor van Thurssen's offer.'

Florina was feeling reckless; it didn't matter any more what she said, in a day or two she would be gone and probably he hoped that once back in Holland she would find work and stay there.

'You would like me out of the way?' She spoke with deliberate flippancy.

'Exactly, Florina.' He sat back in his chair, staring at her. 'You have no objection to going?'

'I think it is a marvellous idea.' She met his eyes, her own wide, holding back tears.

'I'll get Jolly to drive you back to Wheel House tomorrow so that you can pack your things; he will fetch you back in two days time so that you can travel with Doctor van Thurssen. Can you be ready to drive to the hospital with me in the morning—just before eight o'clock—so that you can meet him?'

'Certainly, Sir William. Would you be kind enough to write me a reference?'

He looked surprised, so she added woodenly, 'So that I can get another job.' She got up. 'If there is nothing else to discuss I should like to go to bed, Sir William.'

He got up at once and opened the door, bidding her goodnight in a calm fashion, they might have been discussing the menu for a dinner party. She went up to her room and sat down on the bed, a prey to a thousand and one thoughts, none of them at all pleasant. She had been so intent on preserving a cool front that she had forgotten to ask exactly what she would be expected to do—and was she to be paid or was this doctor merely doing Sir William a good turn? And for how long? Until this other girl came back? And then what? She could always go and stay with Tante Minna, but if she did that she would have to see Felix. Supposing she had refused Sir William's offer, would he have given her notice? There was Pauline to consider too; she was so fond of the child and she thought that Pauline was fond of her. Sir William was behaving strangely; not at all what she would have expected of him. Suddenly the realisation that she wasn't going to see him again once she had left the house was too much for her; there was no point in keeping a stiff upper lip with no one to see it; so she buried her face in the pillows and had a good cry.

She was up early after a night which had been far too long and wakeful, but Sir William was up even earlier, going soft-footed to his small daughter's room. She was awake; he drew the curtains back and sat down on the bed.

'Can you keep a secret?' He wanted to know and when she nodded, he continued, 'Florina is going away, and when I've explained why I think you'll be very pleased . . .'

It didn't take long and when he had finished, 'Not so much as a breath or a hint,' he warned her and submitted to her delighted hug before taking himself off down to his study, where he spent ten minutes or so on the telephone to Nanny. It was breakfast time by then; he was sitting at the table when Florina joined him, to carry on a polite conversation while she pushed food around her plate. He made no mention of their talk of the previous evening, for which she was thankful; she couldn't have borne that.

'I'll drop you off at the main entrance,' he told her as he drove to the hospital, and she nodded silently. In a few minutes now she would bid him goodbye; she had been to Pauline's room before they had left the house but she had said nothing about leaving. She would have to do that presently, after she had seen Doctor van Thurssen, and since she was to leave with Jolly by ten o'clock it would have to be a hurried explanation. Just as well, perhaps.

Sir William drew up at the main doors and got out. 'There's no need . . . I can find my way . . .' She was gabbling while she tried to think of something cool and dignified to say by way of goodbye.

Sir William took no notice, he took her arm and ushered her into the entrance hall and over to the porter's lodge. Here he relinquished his grasp. 'Benson will take you to Doctor van Thurssen.' He nodded to the elderly porter, who came out of his lodge to join them. At least it would make her goodbye more easily said. She put out a hand and had it engulfed in Sir William's firm grasp.

Conscious of Benson's sharp eyes, she said gruffly. 'Goodbye, Sir William. Thank you for arranging everything.' It was a great effort to add, 'I hope you will be very happy.'

She even managed a smile, rather shaky at the corners.

'I'm quite certain that I shall be, Florina.'

He looked at Benson, who said at once, 'This way, miss,' and marched away towards a long passage at the back of the hall, so that she was forced to follow him. It took her every ounce of will-power not to turn round for a last glimpse of Sir William. He hadn't said goodbye, she reflected on a spurt of anger; loving him had been a great waste of time and what a good thing that she was going away—right away, where there would be nothing to remind her of him and perhaps in time she would be able to forget what a fool she had made of herself over him. She went pink with shame just thinking about it, so that when Benson opened a door and ushered her into a large gloomy room he paused to say, 'You're out of breath, miss—I hurried too much, quite red in the face you are.'

Doctor van Thurssen was looking out of one of the windows, although there was nothing to see, only the bare brick walls of a wing of the hospital. He turned round as she went in, a man in his late thirties with sandy hair and a pleasant, rugged face. He was tall and stoutly built and his eyes were a clear light blue. He would be from the north, she guessed, and remembered that she still knew no details of this job which had been thrust upon her.

He shook her briskly by the hand and spoke in Dutch. 'This is very good of you, Miss Payne. I hope you don't feel that you've been rushed into this; my wife really needs someone to help out with the children until our Nanny comes back.'

'I'll be glad to help, but I don't know very much. Where do you live?'

'Do you know Friesland? I have a practice in Hindeloopen, I'm also consultant at the children's hospital in Leeuwarden. We have six children; the youngest is almost two years old, the eldest fourteen. Ellie, who looks after them, will be away for two weeks. I shall be driving back tomorrow, taking the car ferry from Harwich, if you could manage to be ready by then? You will, of course be given your air ticket to return, as to salary...' He mentioned a generous sum and looked at her hopefully.

She liked him; six children seemed a lot, but the older ones wouldn't need much done for them, and presumably there was other help in the house. She agreed at once, glad to have something solid to hold on to in a nebulous future.

She took a taxi back, for time was running out. Back at the house she hurried to Pauline's room, rehearsing suitable things to say, but there was no need; Pauline said cheerfully, 'Daddy told me you were to have a holiday and you are going to Holland. Will you bring me back some of those little almond biscuits—your aunt gave me some?' She flung her arms tightly round Florina's neck. 'I shall miss you but Daddy says you must have some time to yourself because you've had too much on your mind. Were you very lost when Bobby ran away? Daddy said you couldn't see the wood for the trees—it was a nasty wood, wasn't it? All those brambles...'

'Yes, darling. You'll look after Nanny and the animals, won't you?' Florina got up off the bed and bent to kiss Pauline. 'Jolly is waiting for me, I must go...'

'Did you say goodbye to Daddy?'

It was difficult to speak. 'Yes.' She managed to smile as she went.

Jolly hadn't much to say during the drive to Wheel House, and the fact that she was leaving wasn't mentioned. He was a loyal old servant and she would have been surprised if he had referred to it. But he was kind and helpful and she believed him when he said that both he and Mrs Jolly would miss her, but that wasn't until the next morning, after she had packed her things, arranged for most of them to be sent to her father's house, and bidden Nanny goodbye. Nanny had had very little to say and Florina had been rather hurt over her lack of concern for her future. She had been kind and had fussed around Florina, and she and Jolly did everything to help her, but they hadn't expressed any interest in her future. She thought sadly that even Pauline hadn't minded overmuch. She had got up early and stripped her bed and left the room tidy, reflecting that she wouldn't be missed and would certainly be quickly forgotten in the bustle of the forthcoming wedding.

Her father, when she had walked through the village to see him, had said in a satisfied voice, 'I told you so, didn't I? But you knew best, and look where it's landed you. You'd better find yourself work in Holland, for I can't afford to keep you.'

They were to drive to the hospital where she was to meet Doctor van Thurssen, and as Jolly helped her out of the car and carried her case into the entrance hall she looked around, longing to see Sir William just once more, but no one was there. She said goodbye to Jolly and sat down to wait.

Doctor van Thurssen came presently and they went out to his car. It was parked in the consultants' car park and the Bentley was beside it; there was no one in it, of course. If she had turned her head and looked up at the windows of the children's ward she would have seen Sir William standing at one of them, watching her. It was only when Doctor van Thurssen had driven away that he turned back to resume his round of his little patients.

If Florina had been happier, she would have enjoyed the journey to Hindeloopen. They had caught the midday ferry, arriving at the Hoek in the evening, and then driving north, to arrive some four hours later at his home. It was dark by then and she was hungry, for they had stopped only long enough to eat a sandwich and drink coffee, and the sight of the brightly lit house on the edge of the little town was very welcome. A welcome echoed by Mevrouw van Thurssen, who greeted her warmly, took her to her room, bade her take off her outdoor things and return downstairs for her supper.

The room was pleasant, nicely furnished and large and the bed looked inviting. She was very tired, but she was hungry too. She went back downstairs and was ushered into a lofty dining-room, furnished with a massive square table and solid chairs, given a glass of sherry and told kindly to sit herself down at the table. Supper was all that a hungry girl could have wished for, and while they ate Mevrouw van Thurssen outlined her duties.

'Of course, the older children go to school, but Lisa, the youngest, is at home. Saska—she's five—goes to *Kleuterschool* in the mornings, and Jan and Welmer go to the *Opleidingschool* here—they are seven and ten—and then Olda and Sebo both go to Bolsward each day. Either the doctor or I drive them there and back——' she hesitated. 'I don't suppose you drive? Of course, Ellie has a licence, so she was able to take them sometimes . . .'

'Yes, I've an international licence and I brought it with me. I drove quite a bit when I came to Holland with my mother, although that is some years ago.'

They beamed at her. 'How fortunate we are in having you, Florina—may I call you that? Now, I am sure that you are tired. In the morning you shall meet the children, and perhaps if you come with me to Bolsward you can see where the schools are? Lutsje can take Saska to school and look after Lisa while we are away. Perhaps we could do as Ellie and I do? One of us goes to Bolsward and the other takes Saska to her school and takes Lisa at the same time in the pushchair.'

In bed, Florina closed her eyes resolutely. She had plenty to think about until she went to sleep, and in the morning she would feel quite different; she had turned a page in her life and she wasn't going to look back at it. After all, she was quite at home in Holland; Friesland was a little different perhaps, but she had slipped back into Dutch again without any effort, it should be easy enough to get a job and it didn't matter where... Here her good resolutions were forgotten; she went back over her day and wished herself back in England, at Wheel House, cooking something delicious for Sir William who would come into the kitchen and say hello in his calm fashion. She wondered if he had missed her—just as a cook, of course—but probably by now Wanda had already engaged a French chef...

He had seemed almost relieved to see her go. 'Oh, William,' she mumbled into the pillow. She cried a little then, until at last she slept.

There was little time to think in the morning; the entire family breakfasted together before Doctor van Thurssen went to his surgery, and then, with Lisa left in the care of Lutsje, who would take Saska to school, Florina got into the family estate car with the two elder children and was driven to Bolsward. Olda and Sebo were at different schools; their mother dropped them off and turned for home. 'If you take them tomorrow,' she suggested, 'I could to go to Sneek in the morning. And perhaps you would fetch Saska at midday?'

After that the day flew past. The household was well run; Mevrouw van Thurssen had plenty of help, but there was always something or someone in need of attention, and the day had a certain routine which had to be kept. The family was a happy one and close-knit, and she was kept busy until she had helped put Lisa and Saska to bed. After supper, she helped Welmer with his English lessons. When the children were in bed, she sat for a while with the doctor and his wife, drinking a last cup of coffee before going to her own bed. She was tired by then, too tired to think clearly about her own affairs. In a day or two, she promised herself, she would decide what she was going to do. She slept on the thought.

A week went by and she was no nearer a decision; by now she had become involved in the life of the Thurssen family; the children liked her; she worked hard, cooked when there was no one else to do it, sewed, bathed the smaller children, ferried the older ones to and from school and helped out with their homework in the evenings. But it wasn't all work; at the weekend they had all crammed into the estate car and spent the day on board the doctor's yacht which he kept moored at Sneek—the weather had been fine, if a little chilly, and Florina had enjoyed every minute of it.

On the way back, Olda, sitting beside her, said, 'We like our Ellie, but I wish you could stay with us too.'

It brought Florina up with a jolt. Ellie was due back in a week and she had done nothing about her future. It was a question of whether she should stay in Holland, get a work permit and find a job, or go back to England. She had a little money saved, enough to live on for a week or two while she found work. London, she supposed, where there were hotels and big private houses where cooks were employed; it seemed sensible to go there. At the very back of her mind was the thought that if she went there to work, she might, just might, see Sir William; not to speak to, of course. She was aware that this was a terribly stupid wish on her part; the quicker she forgot him the better. If she went to see her father she would have to take care to do so during the week when Sir William wouldn't be at Wheel House.

It was all very well to make good resolutions, but she was never free from his image beneath her eyelids and, however busy she was, he popped up in the back of her head, ready to fill her thoughts. All day and every day she was wondering what he was doing, and that evening, pleading tiredness after their outing, she went to bed as soon as the last of the children had settled down for the night. But she didn't sleep, she lay picturing him at Wheel House, sitting in his lovely drawing-room with the mill stream murmuring and Wanda with him, looking gorgeous and dressed to kill.

She was quite wrong; he was indeed in his drawing-room and Wanda was with him, not sitting but storming up and down the room, stuttering with bad temper. He had, for his own purposes, taken her for a walk that afternoon; a long walk along bridle paths and over fields of rough grass, circumventing ploughed fields and climbing any number of gates. All the while he had talked cheerfully about the pleasures of the country. 'We'll come every weekend,' he assured her, 'and spend any free days that I have here. I must get you a bike, it's marvellous exercise. You'll feel years younger.'

Wanda, her tights laddered, stung by nettles and unsuitably shod in high heels, almost spat at him; she would have argued with him but she had needed all her breath to keep up with his easy stride.

'Just wait until we get back,' she told him furiously. And she had had to wait until they had dined—rather sketchily because Nanny and Mrs Deakin were good plain cooks with small repertoires. Wanda had suggested getting a cordon bleu cook, but Sir William had said easily that there was no hurry, and when she had pointed out that there was no reason why they shouldn't marry within the next week or so, he hadn't been in a hurry about that either; he had a backlog of theatre cases and an overflowing outpatients' clinic. An unsettling remark, since she had spread it around that they were marrying shortly.

Wanda glared at his broad back now and wondered if it was worth it—he was successful and rich and handsome, everything a girl such as herself expected of a husband; he was also proving tiresomely stubborn. She allowed herself to reflect upon the American millionaire William had introduced her to only that very week. Now, there was a man eminently suitable; possessed of oil wells that never required his presence, able to live wherever fancy took him; a real lover of bright lights. He had sent her flowers and she had half promised to see him again; after all, William was so seldom free and, if he was, he liked to have a quiet evening at home.

In the drawing-room, drinking Mrs Deakin's instant coffee, she allowed bad temper to get the better of her good sense. 'This is the worst weekend I've ever had to spend,' she raged. 'This coffee is unspeakable and I'll tell you now, William, I will not live here, not even for weekends. You can sell the place, I hate it.'

Sir William swallowed some more coffee and thought of Florina. 'No, I don't wish to see it sold, Wanda. In fact I'm thinking of taking on less work and spending more time here.'

She came to a halt in front of him. 'You mean that? You really mean it?'

'Oh, yes, I would like to enjoy my wife and children, and I would need to have more time for that.'

'But you're at the top of your profession—you're well known, you know everyone who matters.'

'I begin to think that the people who matter to you aren't those who matter to me, Wanda.'

She stamped her foot. 'I want some fun, I want to go out dancing and have parties and buy pretty clothes.'

He said thoughtfully, 'When we first met, you told me that you wanted to have a home of your own—you even mentioned children...'

'Well, I found you attractive and I wanted to impress you, I suppose. I must say, William, you have changed. If I marry you, will you send Pauline to boarding-school and get rid of that awful old Nanny and give up this dump? We could have such fun in London; you would have much more time to go out if you didn't have to come racing down here all the time.'

He looked at her from under half closed lids and said mildly, 'No, Wanda, I won't do any of those things.'

'Then don't expect me to!' she shouted at him, as she tugged the diamond ring off her finger and threw it at him. 'I'm going to bed and you can drive me back in the morning. I never want to see you again! All these months wasted...'

She flung out of the room and Sir William went to the side table poured himself a whisky and sat down again. He was smiling to himself—quite a wicked smile. Presently he went into his study and picked up the telephone.

It was Florina's last day; Ellie would be back in the morning. She had packed her case, telephoned a surprised Tante Minna, done the daily chores she had come to enjoy so much and now she was sitting on the side of Lisa's cot reading her a bedtime story. It was when the child gave a sudden chortle that she paused to look up from the book. Doctor van Thurssen had walked into the night nursery and with him was Sir William.

Florina's voice faltered and died. She made no answer to the doctor's 'Good evening' as he picked his small daughter up from her cot and sat her on his lap. She had no breath for that. She could only stare at Sir William and gulp her heart back where it belonged.

'Is it not convenient?' observed Doctor van Thurssen cheerfully. 'Here is Sir William come to fetch you home.'

She was on her feet, wild ideas of escape mixed with delight at seeing him again. She must be firm, she told herself, and cool and matter-of-fact. She said, in a voice she strove to keep just that, 'I have arranged to go to my aunt.'

Sir William crossed the room towards her and she retreated a few steps, which she realised, too late, was silly; the door was further away than ever. Moreover, there was only the wall behind her and he had fetched up so close to her that she had only to stretch out her hands to touch him. She clasped them prudently and kept her eyes on his waistcoat.

He said in his placid voice, but this time edged with steel, 'I shall take you home, Florina, where you belong.' And Doctor van Thurssen, who had been tucking his small daughter back into her cot, capped this with a brisk, 'Most satisfactory—it could not be better for you, Florina.' And while she was still trying to frame a watertight argument against it, he swept them both downstairs.

Somehow, for the rest of the evening, Florina was thwarted from her purpose to be alone with Sir William; she had to tell him that nothing on earth would make her go back to Wheel House with him, but there was no chance, even when, in desperation, as she and Mevrouw van Thurssen were on their way to bed, she tried to interrupt the men's learned discussion about the treatment of childish illnesses; they barely paused to listen to her request for five minutes of Sir William's time. He simply smiled kindly at her and pointed out that they would have plenty of time to talk as they drove back the next day. She had bidden them a stony goodnight and gone upstairs with Mevrouw van Thurssen, fuming silently.

Everyone was at breakfast and everyone talked; there was not the slightest chance of being heard above the cheerful din. She glowered at Sir William, who apparently didn't notice, although his eyes gleamed with amusement behind their lids. It wasn't until goodbyes had been said and she was sitting beside him in the Bentley that she had her chance at last. She had rehearsed what she was going to say for a good deal of the night. Clear, pithy remarks which would leave him no doubt as to her intention to remain in Holland. Unfortunately not one single word came to mind. She blurted out instead, 'I wish to go to Tante Minna...'

'A bit out of our way, but I think we could squeeze in an hour or so—I'd like to get home latish this evening.'

'I'm not going back with you, Sir William,' her voice was waspish and she was horrified to know that she was near to tears.

'For what reason?' He sounded mildly curious.

'You know perfectly well what the reason is.' She felt quite reckless, what did it matter what she said now? He already knew that she loved him. She pursued her train of thought out loud. 'Wanda told you...'

'Why yes, she did, but she told me something I already knew, Florina.'

Florina sniffed. 'Well, then, why do you persist... She won't have me in the house.' She stamped a foot in temper and he laughed softly.

'And you can stop laughing, you know quite well I wanted to get you alone yesterday...'

'Oh, yes, it needed a lot of will-power on my part to prevent it, too.'

'What do you mean?' He skimmed past a huge articulated lorry. 'You are driving very fast.'

'The better to get home, my dear.'

'I'm not your dear.' Really, the conversation was getting her nowhere. 'Sir William, please understand this, I will not come back to Wheel House—Wanda...'

'Let us leave Wanda out of it, shall we? She is not at Wheel House and I think it enormously unlikely that we shall ever meet again—she is enamoured of a wealthy American and they are probably already married!'

Florina digested this in silence. 'You sent me away——' she began.

'My darling girl, consider—it was obvious to everyone—the likelihood of my not marrying Wanda once I had met you became a foregone conclusion. To everyone but you—if I had not sent you away you would probably have spent your time in earnest endeavours to get us to the altar.'

'You mean Wanda doesn't want to marry you? She jilted you?'

'Yes, with a little help from circumstances.'

She cast a quick look at him; he looked smug. 'What did you do?'

'Oh, nothing really—a long country walk, rather a muddy one, I'm afraid—and the nettles at this time of year. Nanny and Mrs Deakin cooked dinner, and I refused to sell Wheel House and live for ever and ever in London.'

They drove for some miles in silence while Florina sorted out her thoughts. There was no reason why she shouldn't go back to Wheel House now. Just once or twice she had felt a rush of pure excitement wondering what he would say next, only he hadn't said anything, and by that she meant he hadn't said that he loved her. But for what other reason would he take all the trouble to fetch her back? Because she was a good cook?

She frowned, staring ahead of her as the car tore along the motorway. Perhaps it would be wiser if she were to stay in Holland. Perhaps he thought that she was suffering from an infatuation which would pass once she was back in her kitchen. She became aware that he was slowing the car into the slow lane and she looked at him.

'If I tell you that I love you—am in love with you, and have been since the moment I saw you, my darling, will you be content to leave it at that until we are home? I can't kiss you adequately in the fast lane, and nothing else will do!' He smiled at her with a tenderness which made her gulp. All she could do was nod, and he reached out and caught her hand for a moment. 'We will marry as soon as it can be arranged. Now sit quiet and think about the wedding cake while I drive.'

She said, 'Yes, William,' in a meek voice, and then, 'I'm sure Tante Minna would understand if we don't go to see her.' Then, because her heart was bursting with happiness, 'I do love you very much, William.'

He was steering back into the fast lane, but he put out a hand and caught one of hers and kissed it.

She was caught up in a lovely dream. They stopped for coffee and a quick lunch and Sir William maintained a gentle flow of talk, although afterwards she was unable to remember a word which had been spoken. When at last he drew up before the door of Wheel House and she saw the lighted windows, she heaved a great sigh of joy. It wasn't a dream, it was all true; she turned a face alight with love and happiness to him as he opened the car door for her. There was such a lot that she wanted to say but all she managed was 'Oh, William!'

He bent and kissed her and then glanced at the house. 'They will be waiting for us,' he observed, 'but first...' He kissed her again, this time at length and lingeringly. 'You'll marry me, my dearest? I can't imagine being without you—you'll have no peace, for I'll want you with me all the time—we'll live in London during the week and come here each weekend...'

'Pauline?'

'I've talked to her; she likes the idea of being a weekly boarder and she can't wait to be your step-daughter. Nanny will stay here.' He kissed her once more. 'You know, I thought just for a while that you had fallen for Felix. I could have killed him with my bare hands...'

She reached up to kiss him in her turn. 'I dislike him intensely,' she assured him vigorously, 'and always did—only it was rather difficult to talk about.' She smiled up at him and his arms tightened around her.

'You're the one I've been waiting for,' he said softly, 'all my life—and now I don't need to wait any longer.' He put up a gentle finger and stroked her face. 'Such a beautiful girl...'

She had thought that she would never be happier, but she saw that she had been mistaken; she was bursting with happiness. William had called her beautiful and, what was more, he meant it.

He opened the door and they went into the house together.

ATTRACTIVE, SPACE SAVING BOOK RACK

Display your most prized novels on this handsome and sturdy book rack. The hand-rubbed walnut finish will blend into your library decor with quiet elegance, providing a practical organizer for your favorite hard-or soft-covered books.

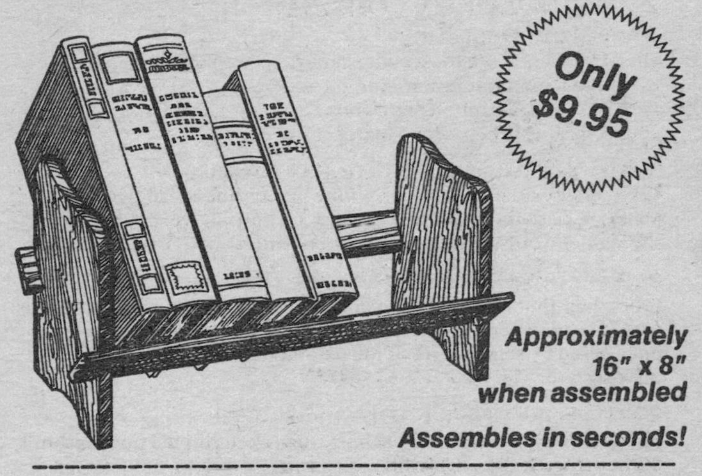

To order, rush your name, address and zip code, along with a check or money order for $10.70* ($9.95 plus 75¢ postage and handling) payable to *Harlequin Reader Service*:

Harlequin Reader Service
Book Rack Offer
901 Fuhrmann Blvd.
P.O. Box 1396
Buffalo, NY 14269-1396

Offer not available in Canada.

*New York and Iowa residents add appropriate sales tax.

BKR-1A

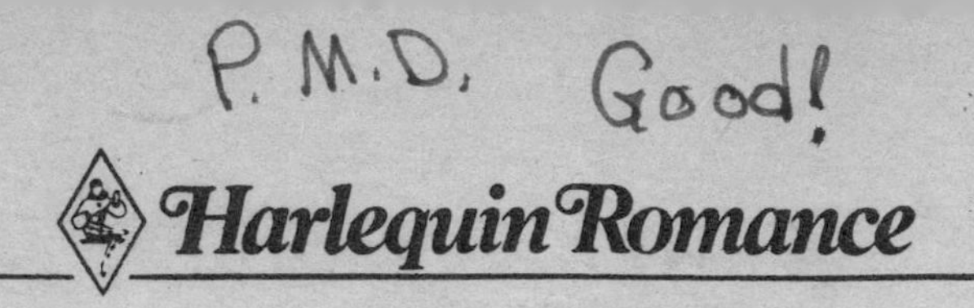
P.M.D. Good!
Harlequin Romance